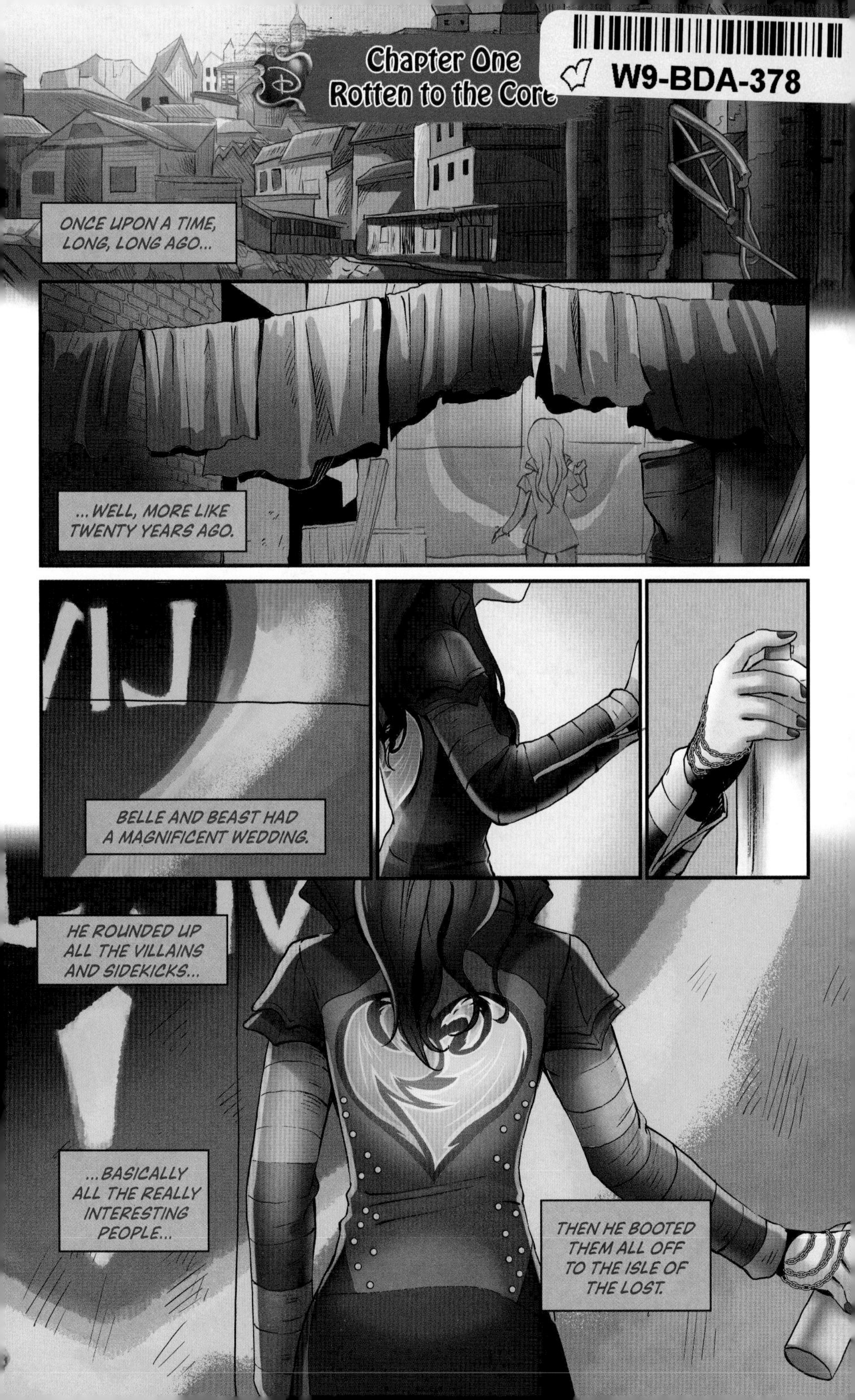
Chapter One
Rotten to the Core
ONCE UPON A TIME, LONG, LONG AGO...
...WELL, MORE LIKE TWENTY YEARS AGO.
BELLE AND BEAST HAD A MAGNIFICENT WEDDING.
HE ROUNDED UP ALL THE VILLAINS AND SIDEKICKS...
...BASICALLY ALL THE REALLY INTERESTING PEOPLE...
THEN HE BOOTED THEM ALL OFF TO THE ISLE OF THE LOST.

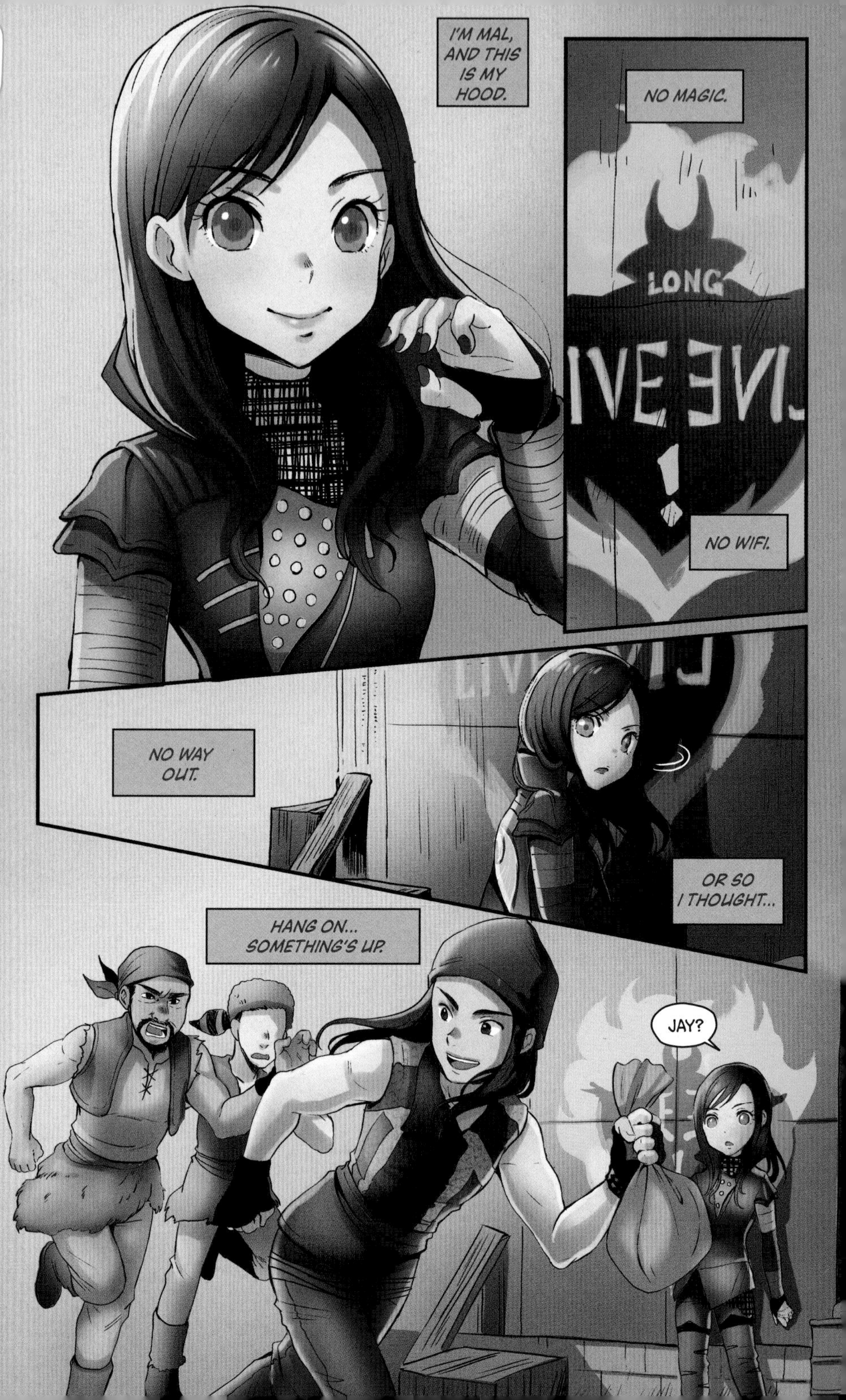
I'M MAL, AND THIS IS MY HOOD.
NO MAGIC.
LONG
NO WIFI.
NO WAY OUT.
OR SO I THOUGHT...
HANG ON... SOMETHING'S UP.
JAY?

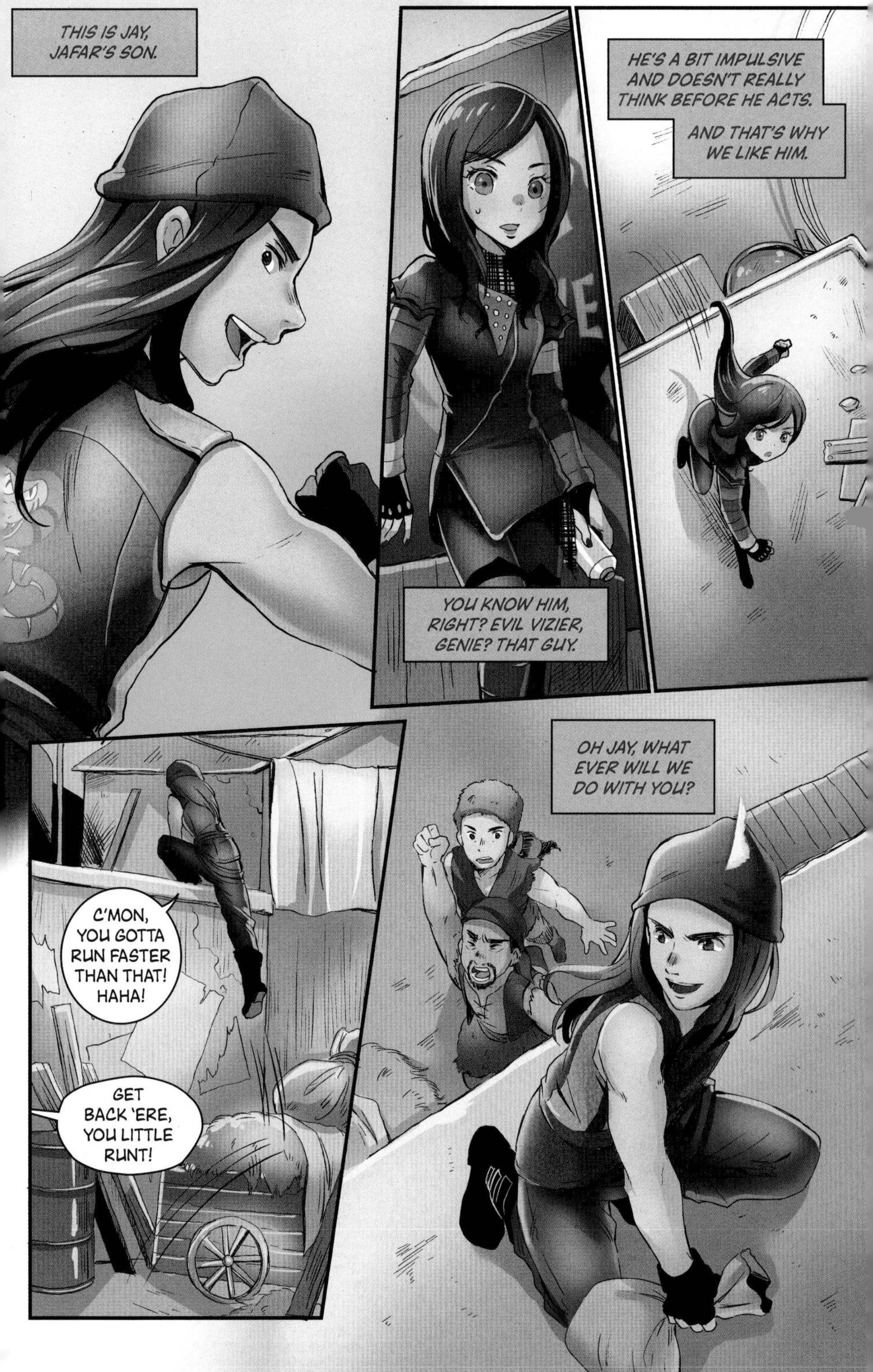
THIS IS JAY, JAFAR'S SON.
YOU KNOW HIM, RIGHT? EVIL VIZIER, GENIE? THAT GUY.
HE'S A BIT IMPULSIVE AND DOESN'T REALLY THINK BEFORE HE ACTS.
AND THAT'S WHY WE LIKE HIM.
C'MON, YOU GOTTA RUN FASTER THAN THAT! HAHA!
GET BACK 'ERE, YOU LITTLE RUNT!
OH JAY, WHAT EVER WILL WE DO WITH YOU?

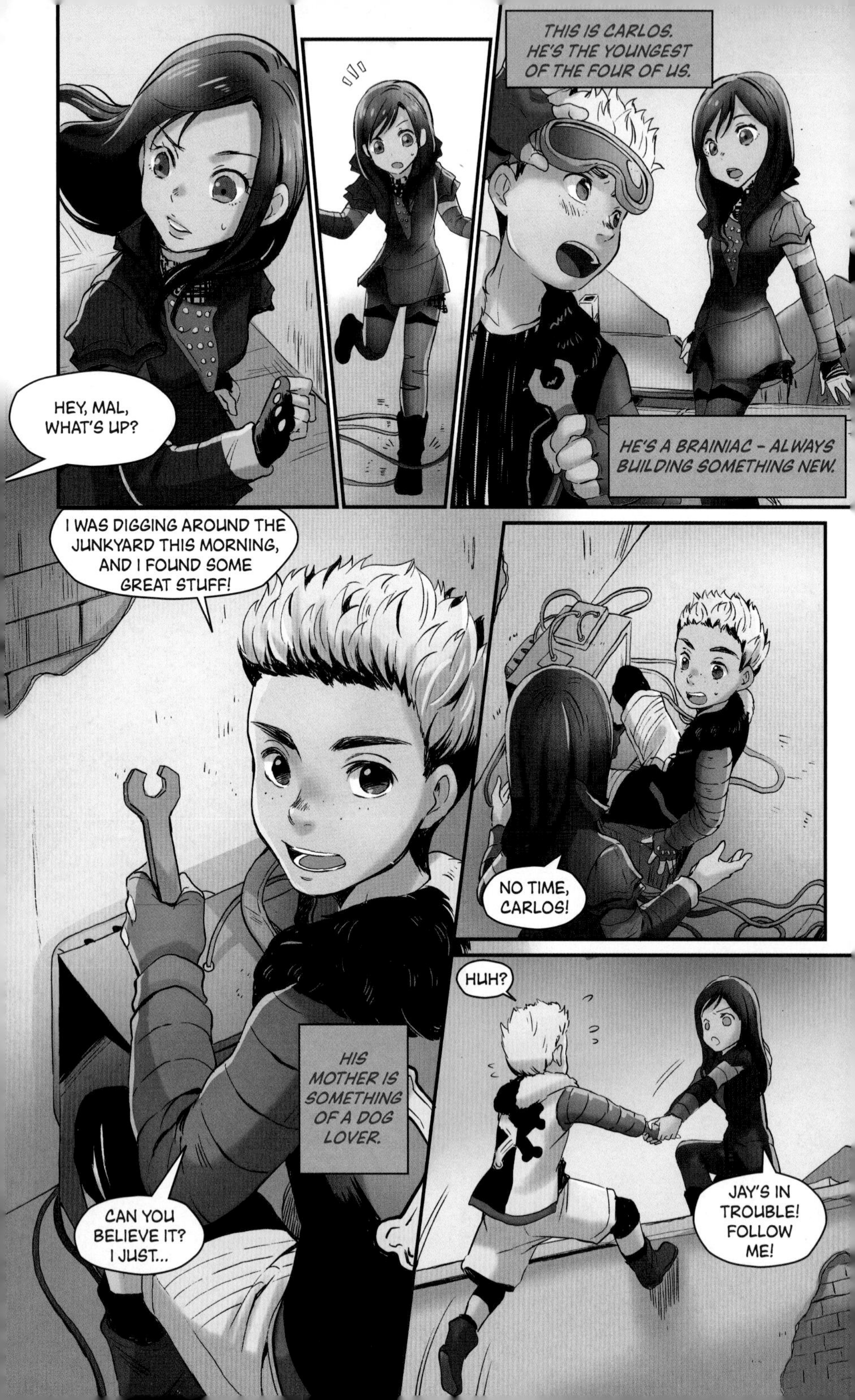
HEY, MAL, WHAT'S UP?
THIS IS CARLOS. HE'S THE YOUNGEST OF THE FOUR OF US.
HE'S A BRAINIAC – ALWAYS BUILDING SOMETHING NEW.
I WAS DIGGING AROUND THE JUNKYARD THIS MORNING, AND I FOUND SOME GREAT STUFF!
HIS MOTHER IS SOMETHING OF A DOG LOVER.
CAN YOU BELIEVE IT? I JUST...
NO TIME, CARLOS!
HUH?
JAY'S IN TROUBLE! FOLLOW ME!

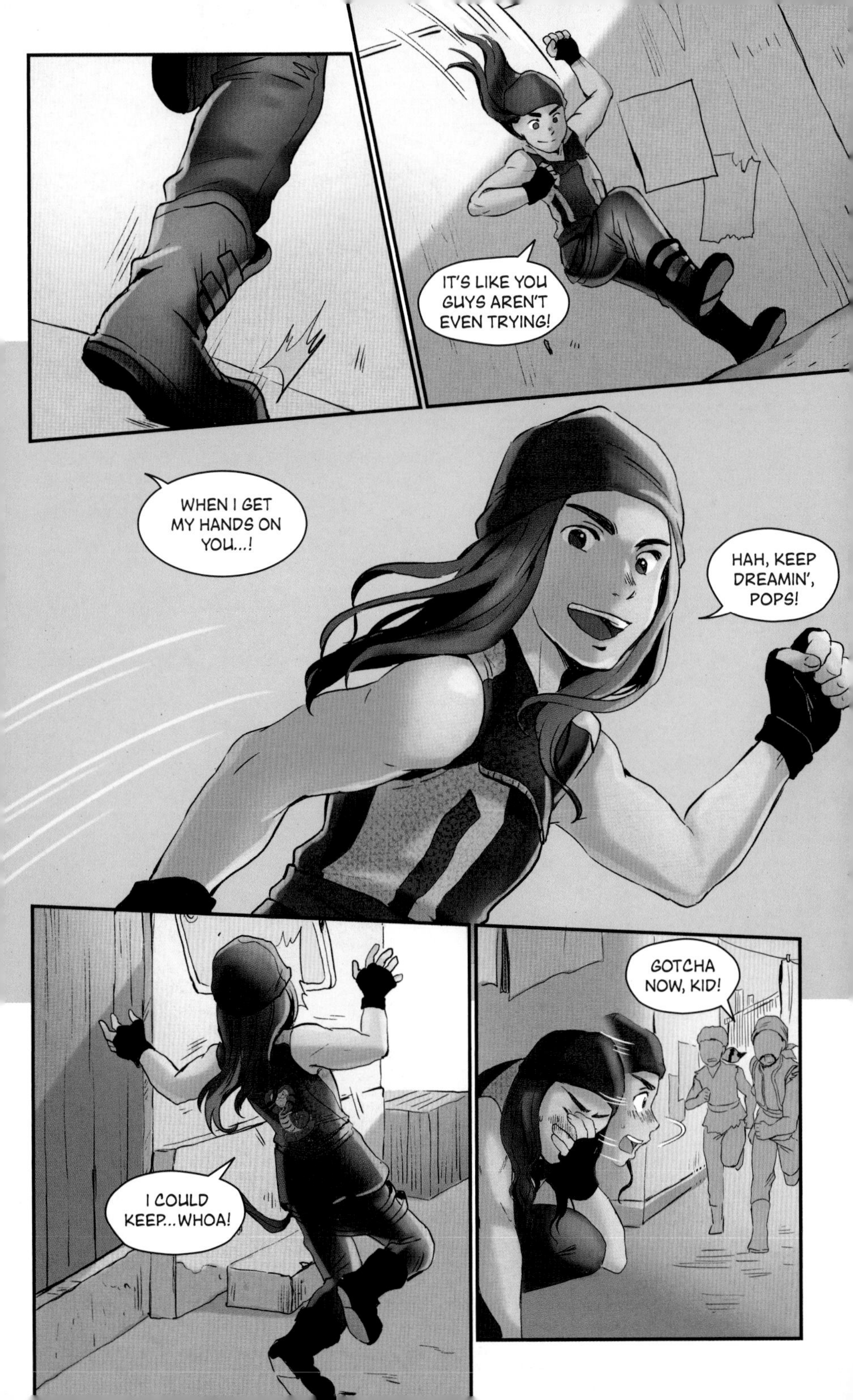
IT'S LIKE YOU GUYS AREN'T EVEN TRYING!
WHEN I GET MY HANDS ON YOU...!
HAH, KEEP DREAMIN', POPS!
I COULD KEEP...WHOA!
GOTCHA NOW, KID!

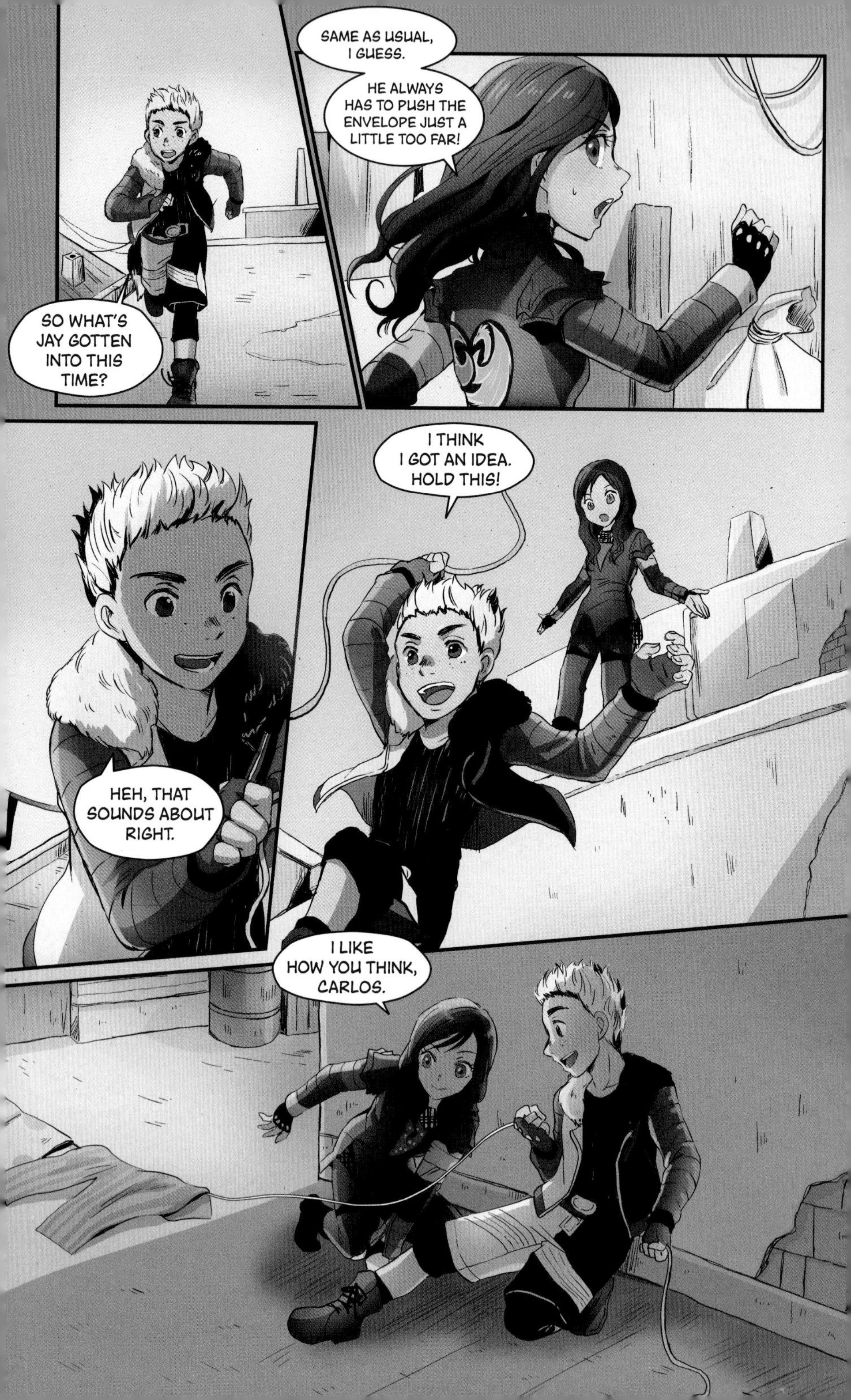
SO WHAT'S JAY GOTTEN INTO THIS TIME?
SAME AS USUAL, I GUESS.
HE ALWAYS HAS TO PUSH THE ENVELOPE JUST A LITTLE TOO FAR!
HEH, THAT SOUNDS ABOUT RIGHT.
I THINK I GOT AN IDEA. HOLD THIS!
I LIKE HOW YOU THINK, CARLOS.

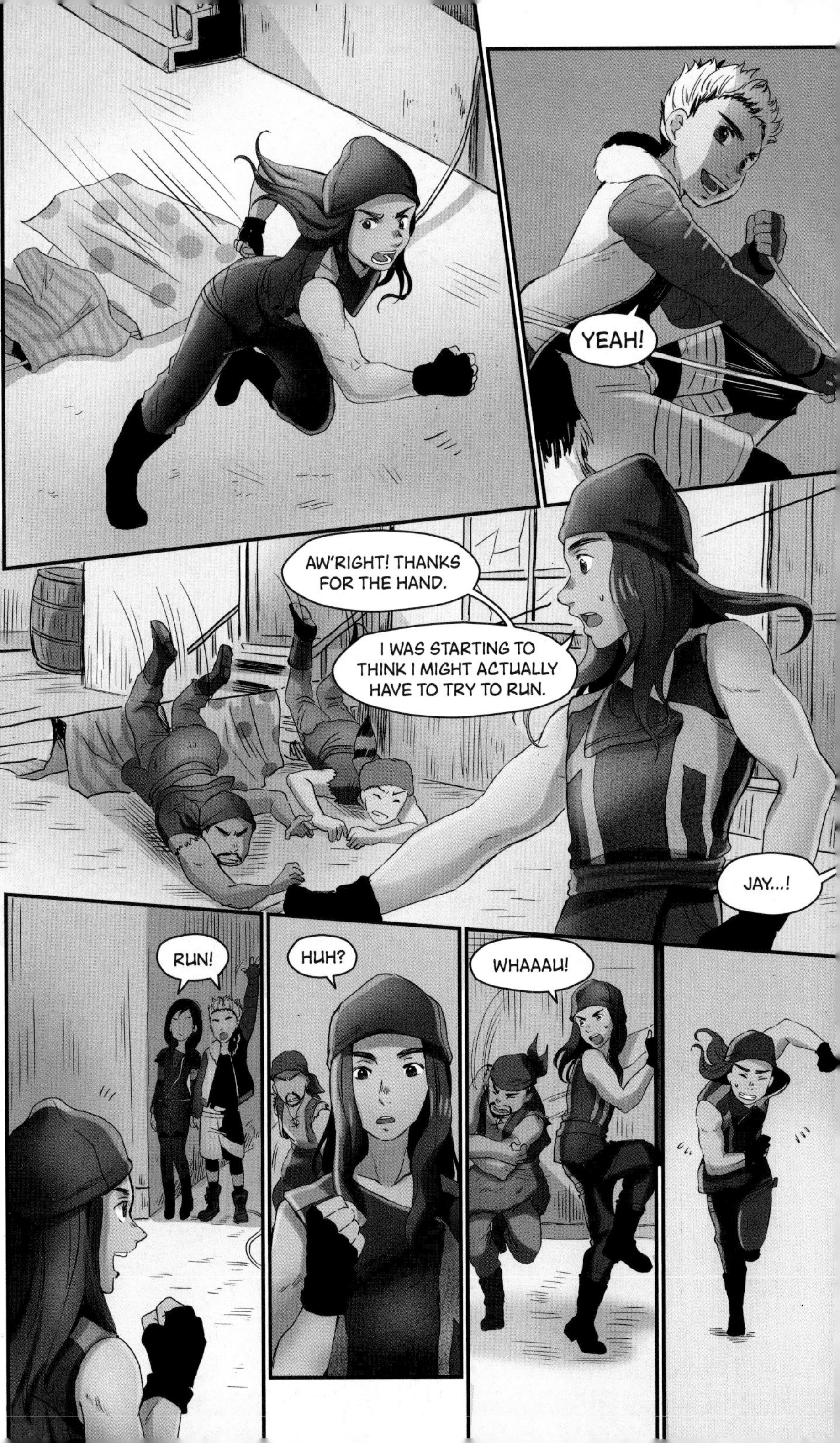
YEAH!
AW'RIGHT! THANKS FOR THE HAND.
I WAS STARTING TO THINK I MIGHT ACTUALLY HAVE TO TRY TO RUN.
JAY...!
RUN!
HUH?
WHAAAU!

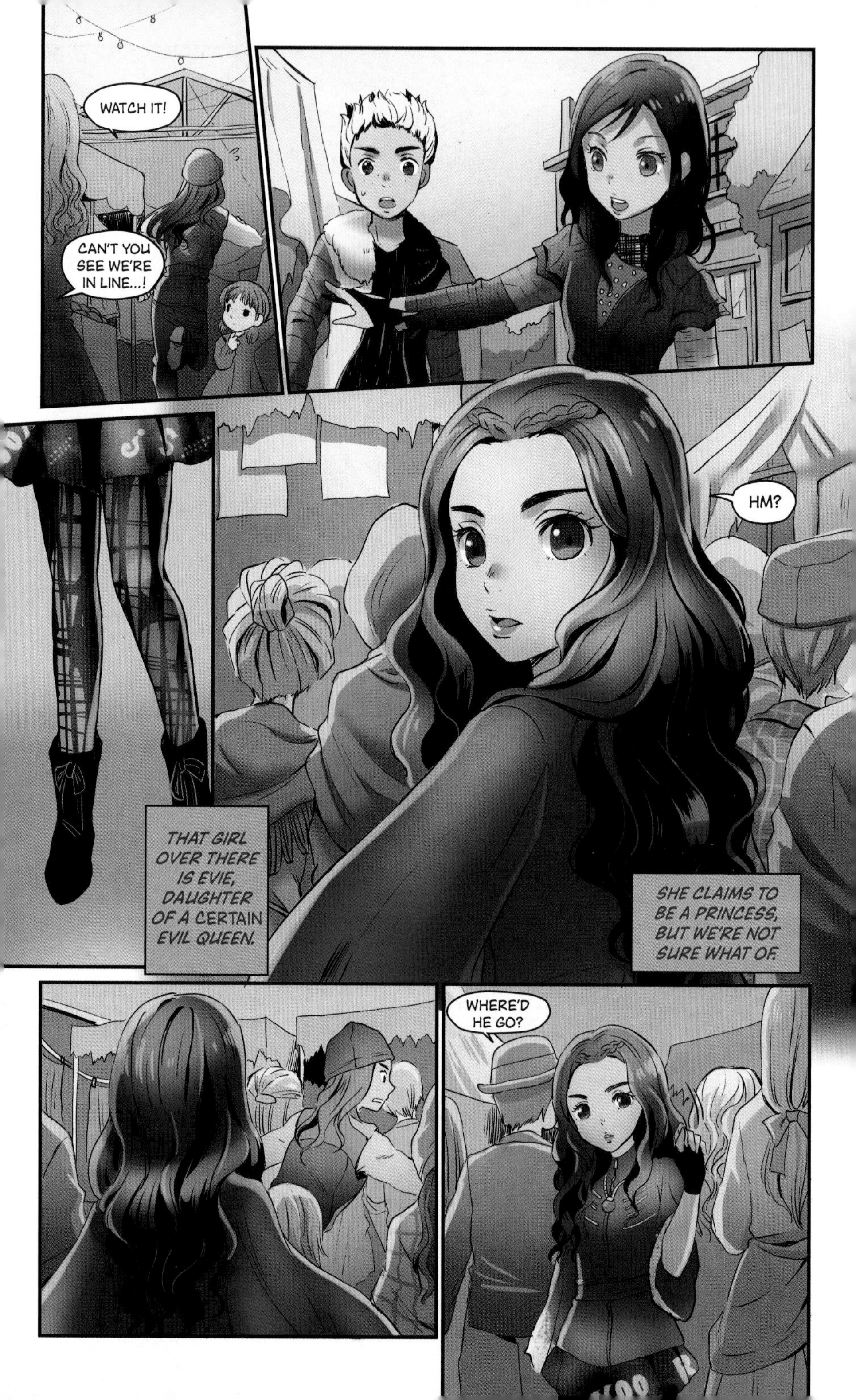
WATCH IT!
CAN'T YOU SEE WE'RE IN LINE...!
HM?
THAT GIRL OVER THERE IS EVIE, DAUGHTER OF A CERTAIN EVIL QUEEN.
SHE CLAIMS TO BE A PRINCESS, BUT WE'RE NOT SURE WHAT OF.
WHERE'D HE GO?

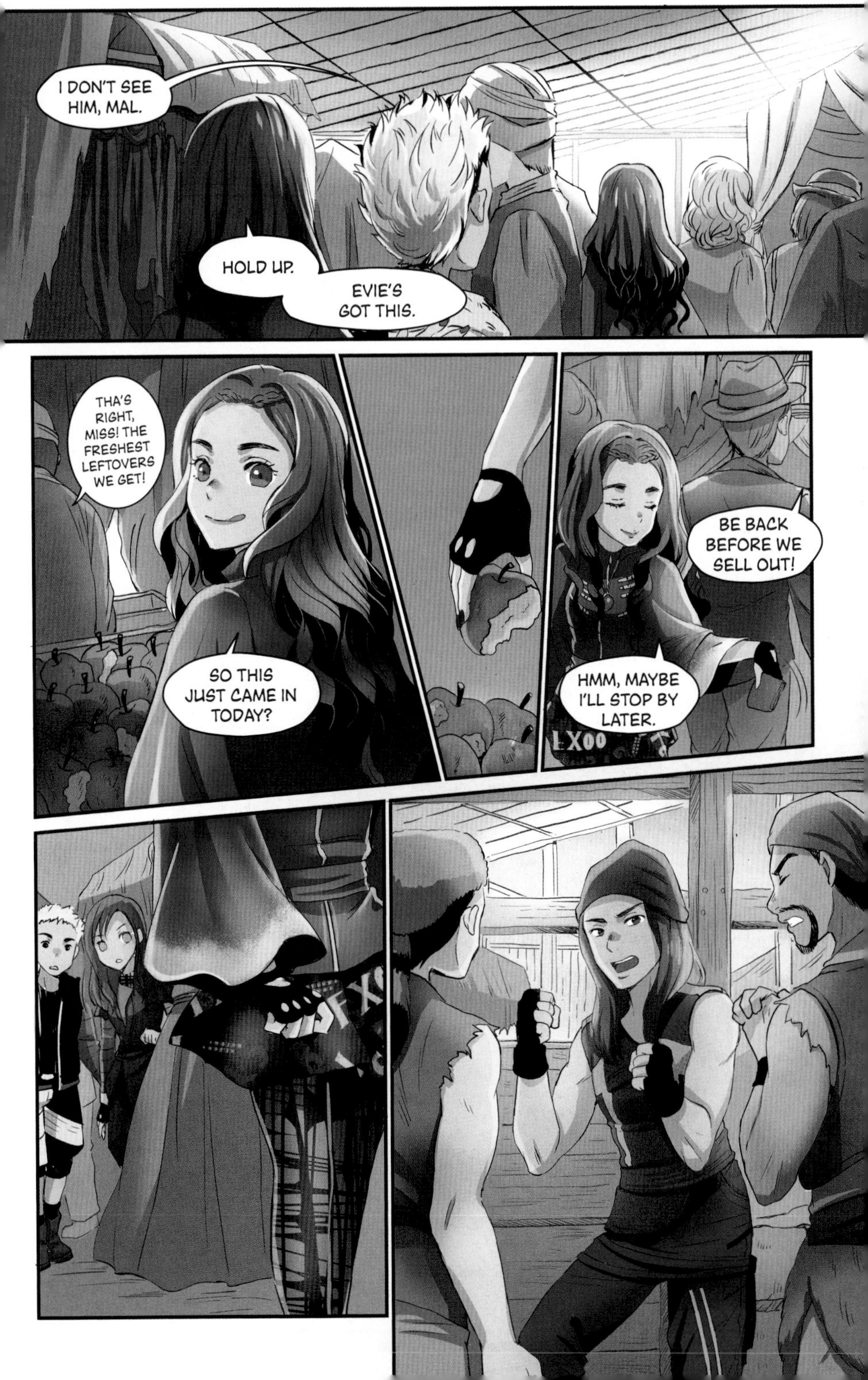
I DON'T SEE HIM, MAL.
HOLD UP.
EVIE'S GOT THIS.
THA'S RIGHT, MISS! THE FRESHEST LEFTOVERS WE GET!
SO THIS JUST CAME IN TODAY?
BE BACK BEFORE WE SELL OUT!
HMM, MAYBE I'LL STOP BY LATER.

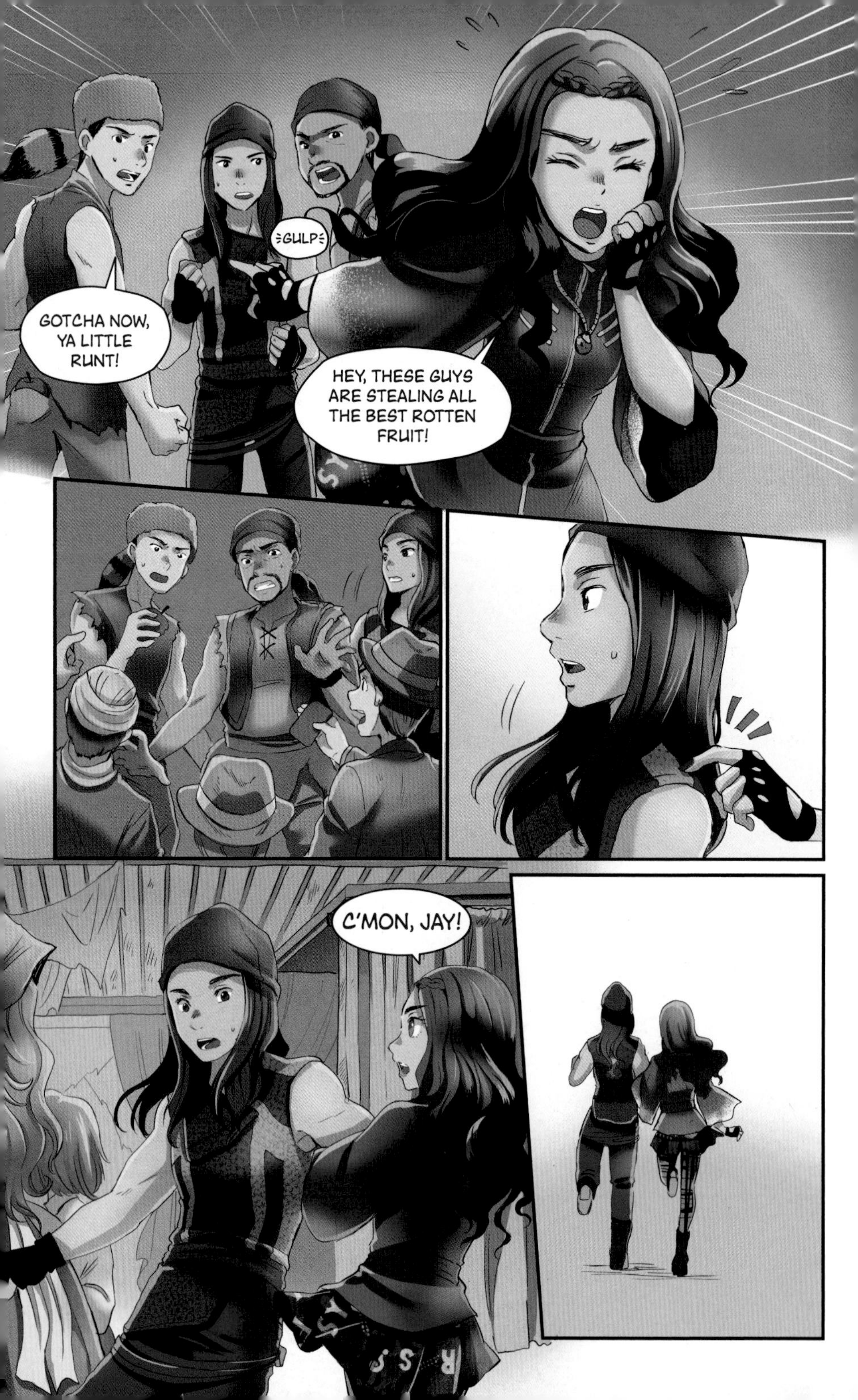
GULP
GOTCHA NOW, YA LITTLE RUNT!
HEY, THESE GUYS ARE STEALING ALL THE BEST ROTTEN FRUIT!
C'MON, JAY!

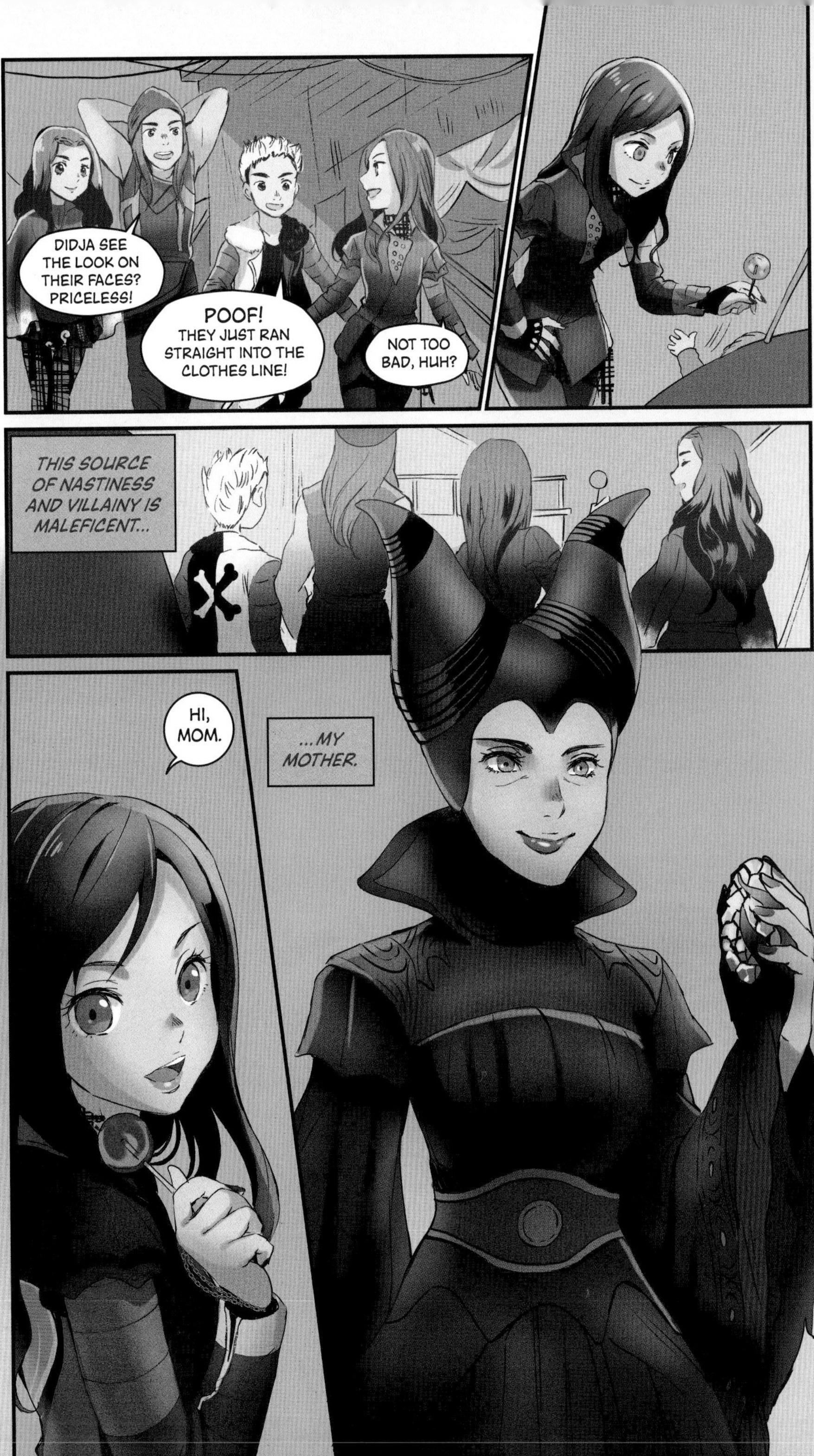
DIDJA SEE THE LOOK ON THEIR FACES? PRICELESS!
POOF! THEY JUST RAN STRAIGHT INTO THE CLOTHES LINE!
NOT TOO BAD, HUH?
THIS SOURCE OF NASTINESS AND VILLAINY IS MALEFICENT...
HI, MOM.
...MY MOTHER.

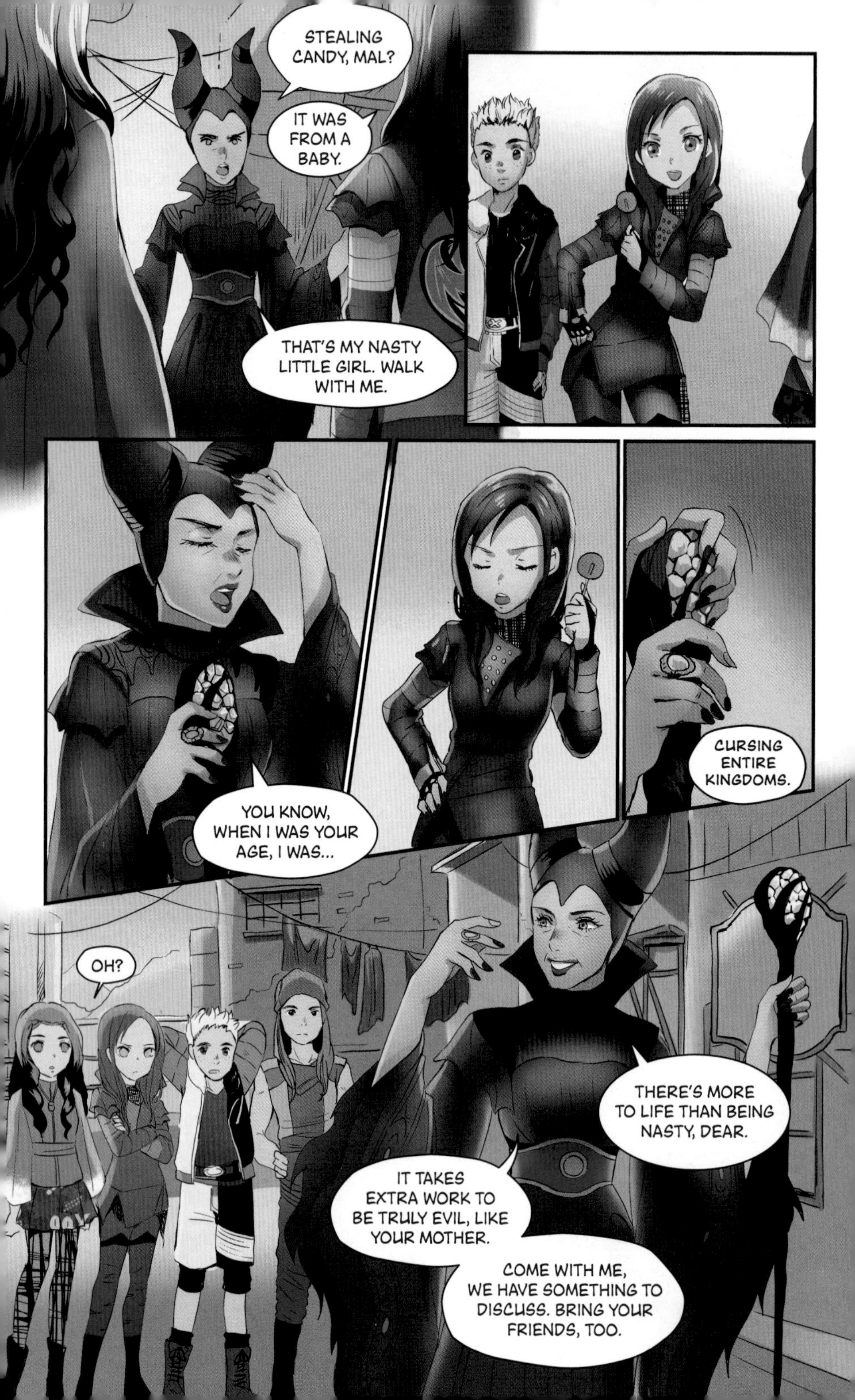
STEALING CANDY, MAL?
IT WAS FROM A BABY.
THAT'S MY NASTY LITTLE GIRL. WALK WITH ME.
YOU KNOW, WHEN I WAS YOUR AGE, I WAS...
CURSING ENTIRE KINGDOMS.
OH?
THERE'S MORE TO LIFE THAN BEING NASTY, DEAR.
IT TAKES EXTRA WORK TO BE TRULY EVIL, LIKE YOUR MOTHER.
COME WITH ME, WE HAVE SOMETHING TO DISCUSS. BRING YOUR FRIENDS, TOO.

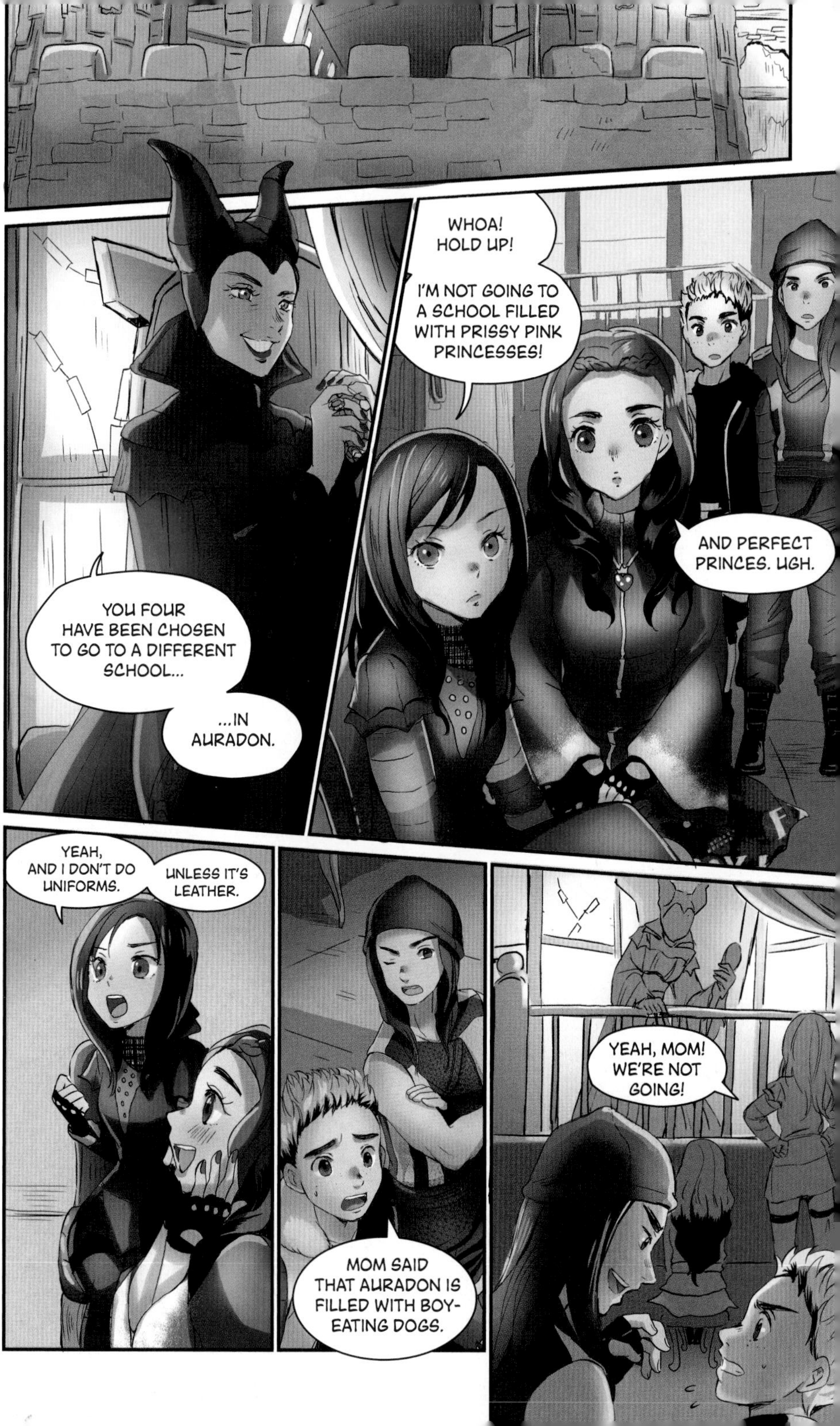
YOU FOUR HAVE BEEN CHOSEN TO GO TO A DIFFERENT SCHOOL...
...IN AURADON.
WHOA! HOLD UP!
I'M NOT GOING TO A SCHOOL FILLED WITH PRISSY PINK PRINCESSES!
AND PERFECT PRINCES. UGH.
YEAH, AND I DON'T DO UNIFORMS.
UNLESS IT'S LEATHER.
MOM SAID THAT AURADON IS FILLED WITH BOY-EATING DOGS.
YEAH, MOM! WE'RE NOT GOING!

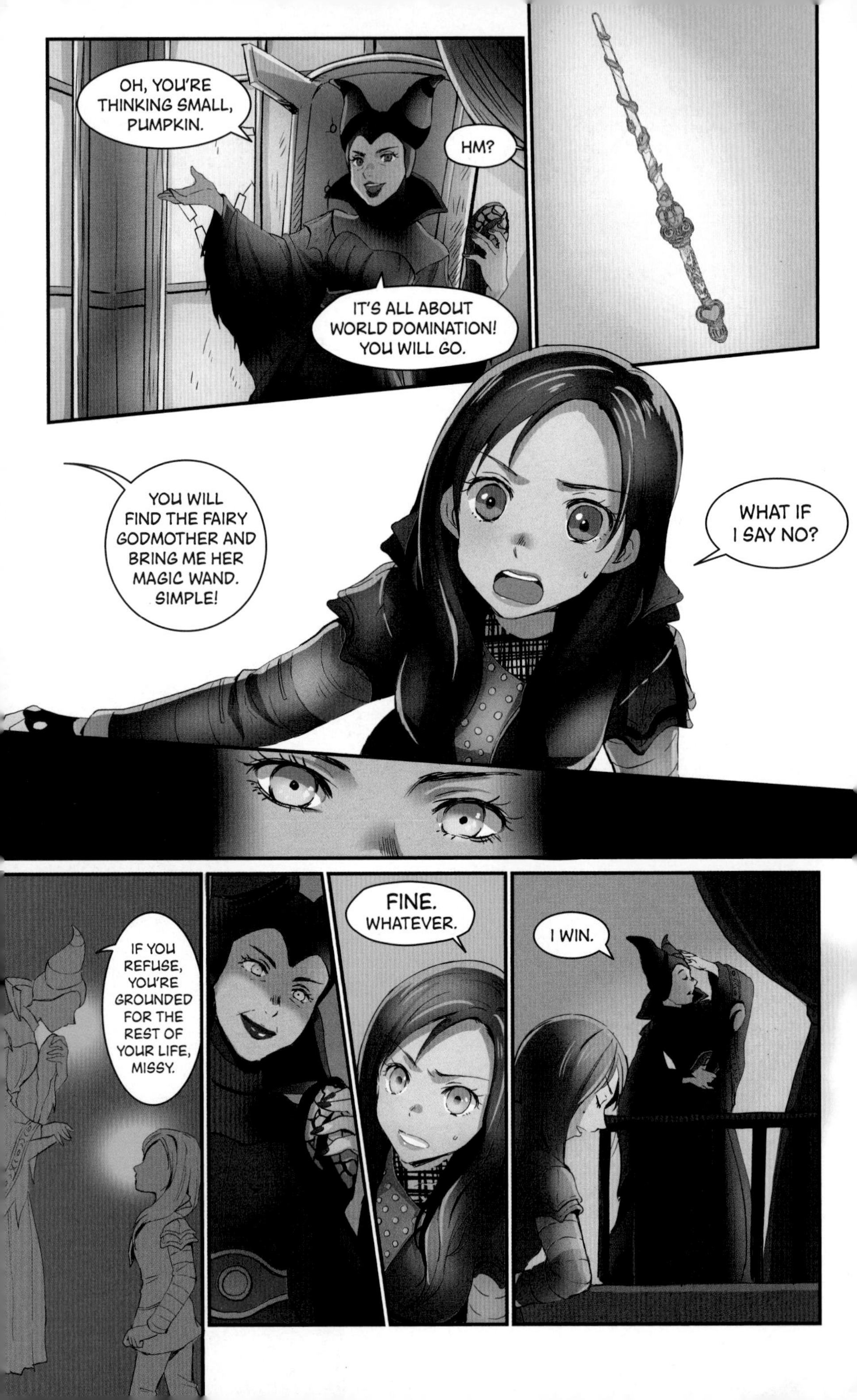
OH, YOU'RE THINKING SMALL, PUMPKIN.
HM?
IT'S ALL ABOUT WORLD DOMINATION! YOU WILL GO.
YOU WILL FIND THE FAIRY GODMOTHER AND BRING ME HER MAGIC WAND. SIMPLE!
WHAT IF I SAY NO?
IF YOU REFUSE, YOU'RE GROUNDED FOR THE REST OF YOUR LIFE, MISSY.
FINE. WHATEVER.
I WIN.

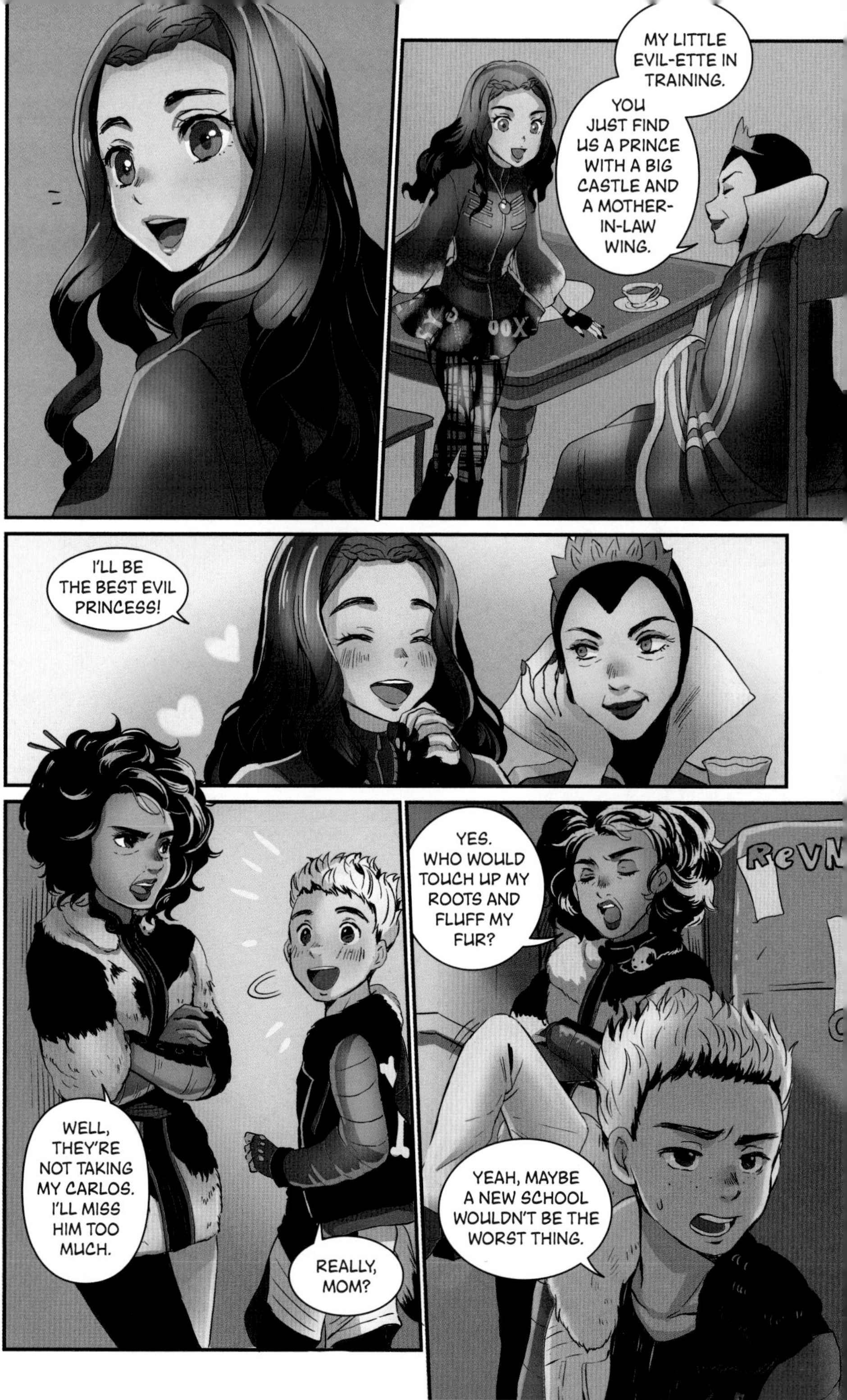
MY LITTLE EVIL-ETTE IN TRAINING.
YOU JUST FIND US A PRINCE WITH A BIG CASTLE AND A MOTHER-IN-LAW WING.
I'LL BE THE BEST EVIL PRINCESS!
WELL, THEY'RE NOT TAKING MY CARLOS. I'LL MISS HIM TOO MUCH.
REALLY, MOM?
YES. WHO WOULD TOUCH UP MY ROOTS AND FLUFF MY FUR?
YEAH, MAYBE A NEW SCHOOL WOULDN'T BE THE WORST THING.

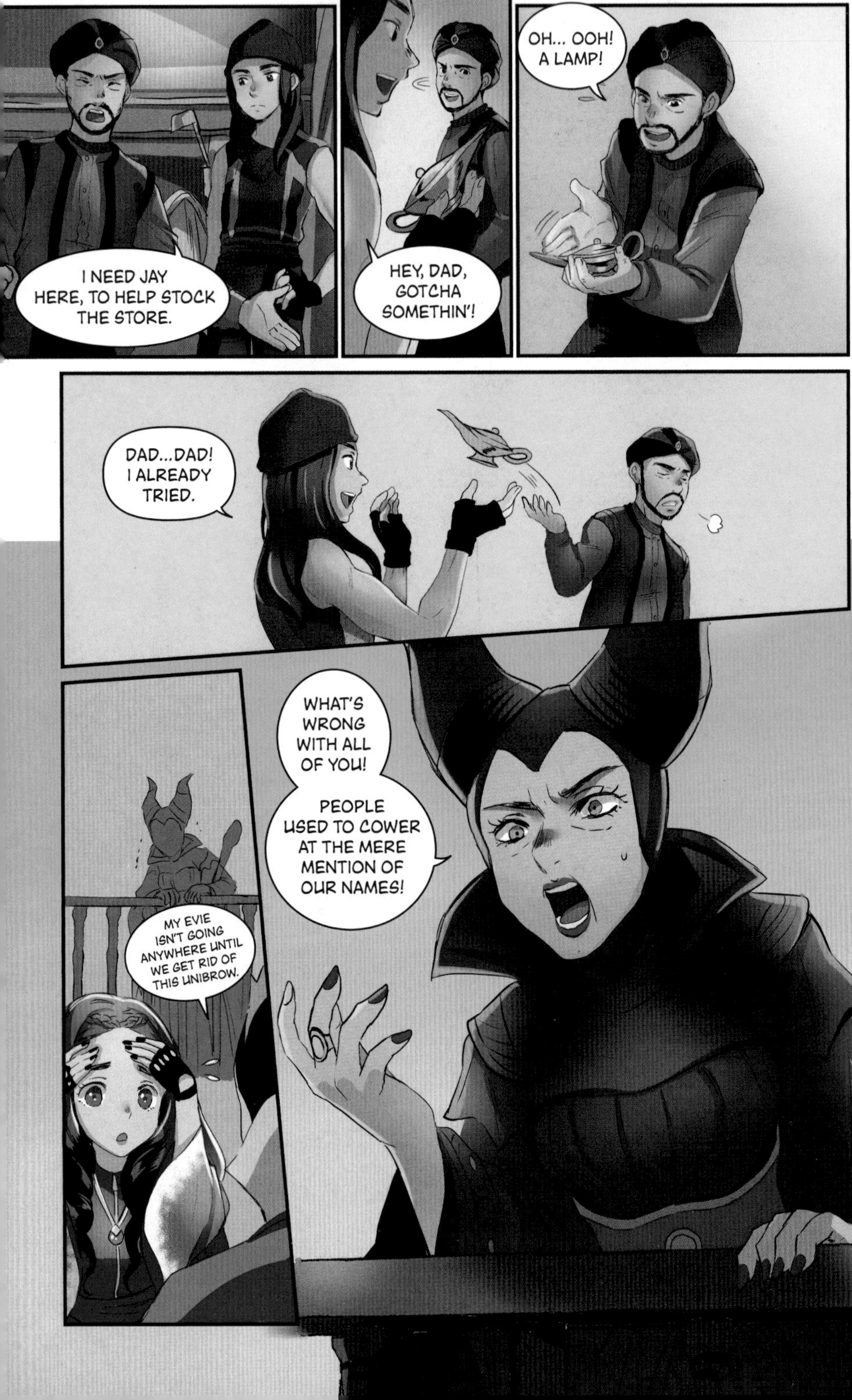
I NEED JAY HERE, TO HELP STOCK THE STORE.
HEY, DAD, GOTCHA SOMETHIN'!
OH... OOH! A LAMP!
DAD...DAD! I ALREADY TRIED.
MY EVIE ISN'T GOING ANYWHERE UNTIL WE GET RID OF THIS UNIBROW.
WHAT'S WRONG WITH ALL OF YOU!
PEOPLE USED TO COWER AT THE MERE MENTION OF OUR NAMES!

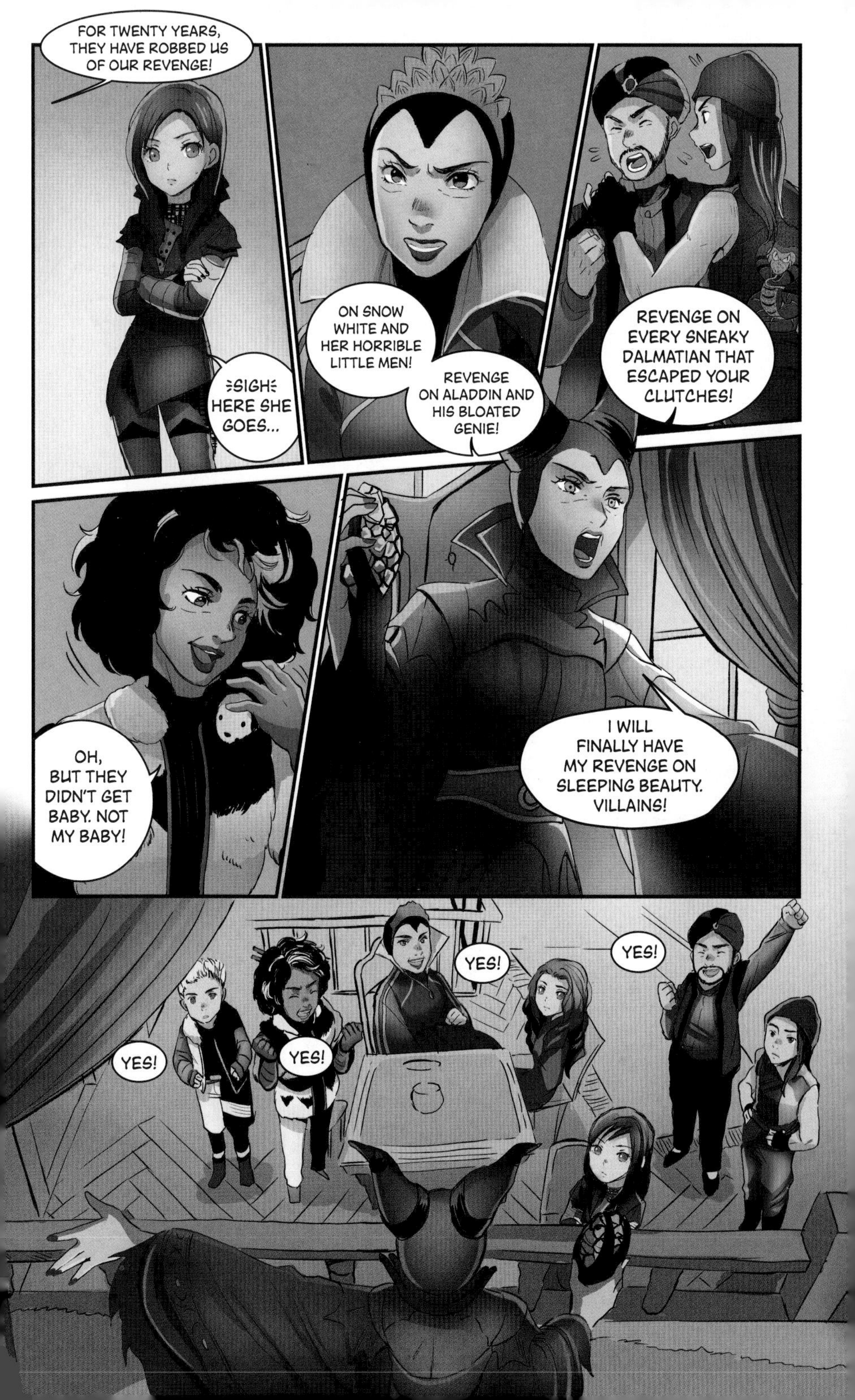
FOR TWENTY YEARS, THEY HAVE ROBBED US OF OUR REVENGE!
⁼SIGH⁼ HERE SHE GOES...
ON SNOW WHITE AND HER HORRIBLE LITTLE MEN!
REVENGE ON ALADDIN AND HIS BLOATED GENIE!
REVENGE ON EVERY SNEAKY DALMATIAN THAT ESCAPED YOUR CLUTCHES!
OH, BUT THEY DIDN'T GET BABY. NOT MY BABY!
I WILL FINALLY HAVE MY REVENGE ON SLEEPING BEAUTY. VILLAINS!
YES!
YES!
YES!
YES!

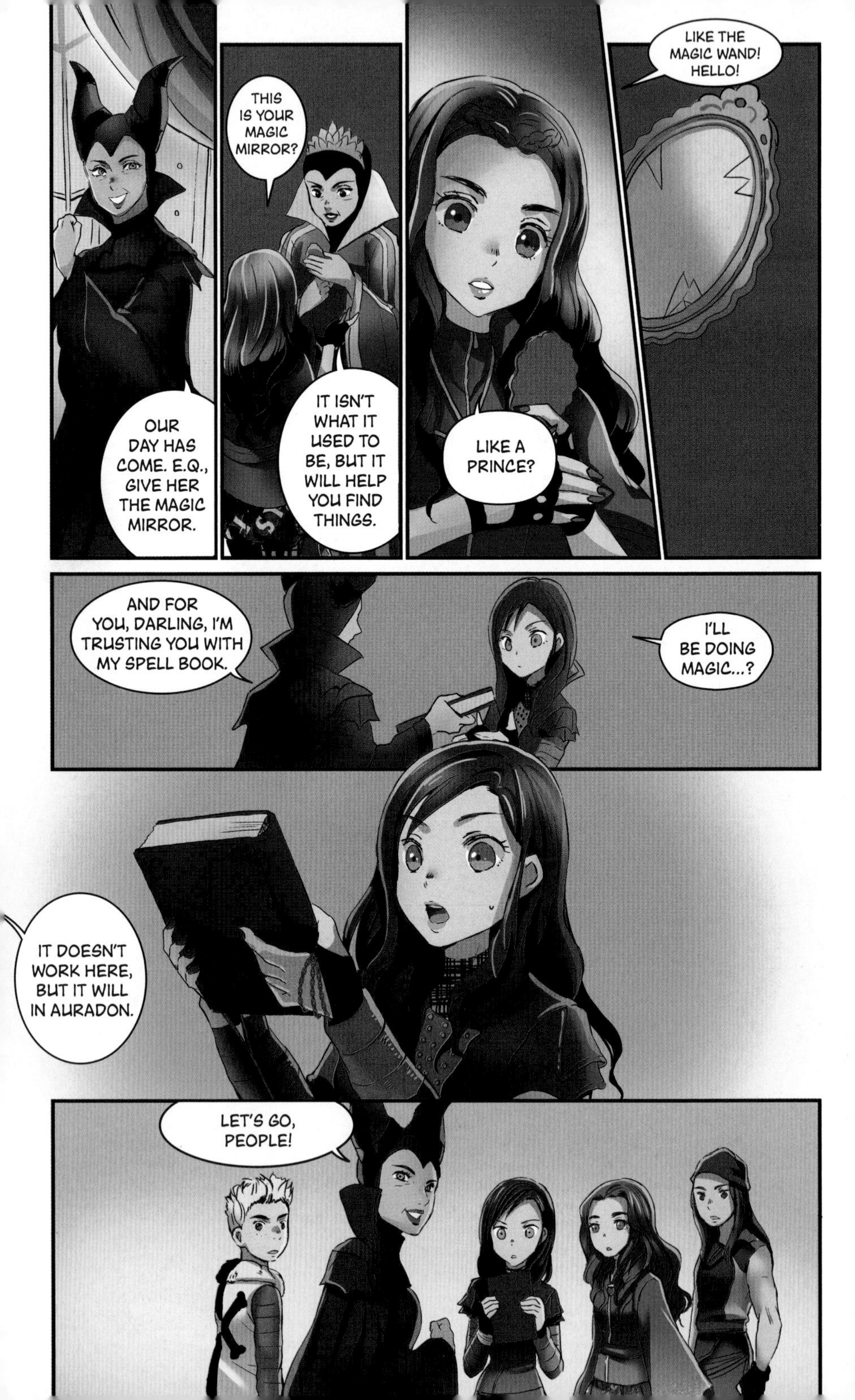
OUR DAY HAS COME. E.Q., GIVE HER THE MAGIC MIRROR.
THIS IS YOUR MAGIC MIRROR?
IT ISN'T WHAT IT USED TO BE, BUT IT WILL HELP YOU FIND THINGS.
LIKE A PRINCE?
LIKE THE MAGIC WAND! HELLO!
AND FOR YOU, DARLING, I'M TRUSTING YOU WITH MY SPELL BOOK.
I'LL BE DOING MAGIC...?
IT DOESN'T WORK HERE, BUT IT WILL IN AURADON.
LET'S GO, PEOPLE!

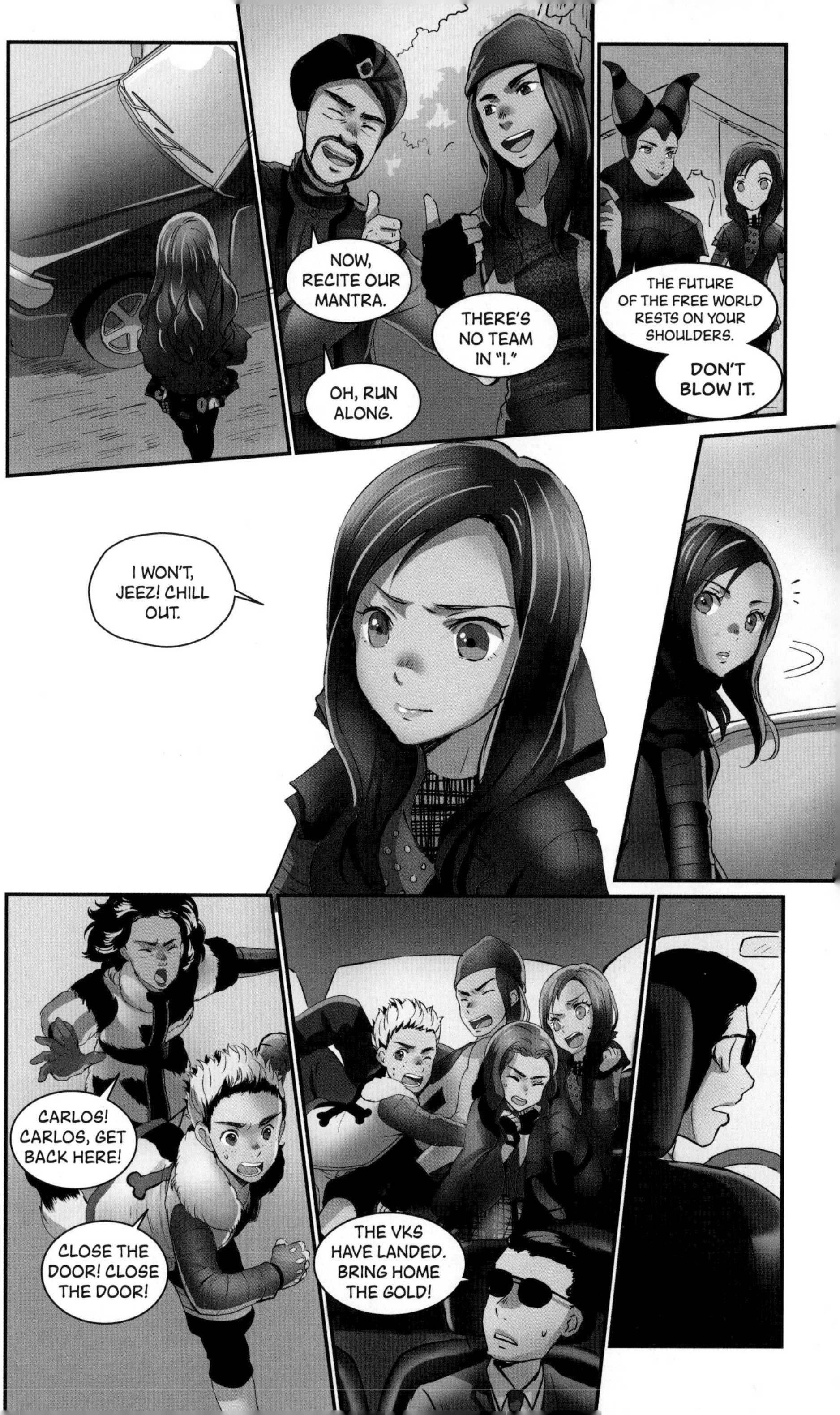
NOW, RECITE OUR MANTRA.
OH, RUN ALONG.
THERE'S NO TEAM IN "I."
THE FUTURE OF THE FREE WORLD RESTS ON YOUR SHOULDERS.
DON'T BLOW IT.
I WON'T, JEEZ! CHILL OUT.
CARLOS! CARLOS, GET BACK HERE!
CLOSE THE DOOR! CLOSE THE DOOR!
THE VKS HAVE LANDED. BRING HOME THE GOLD!

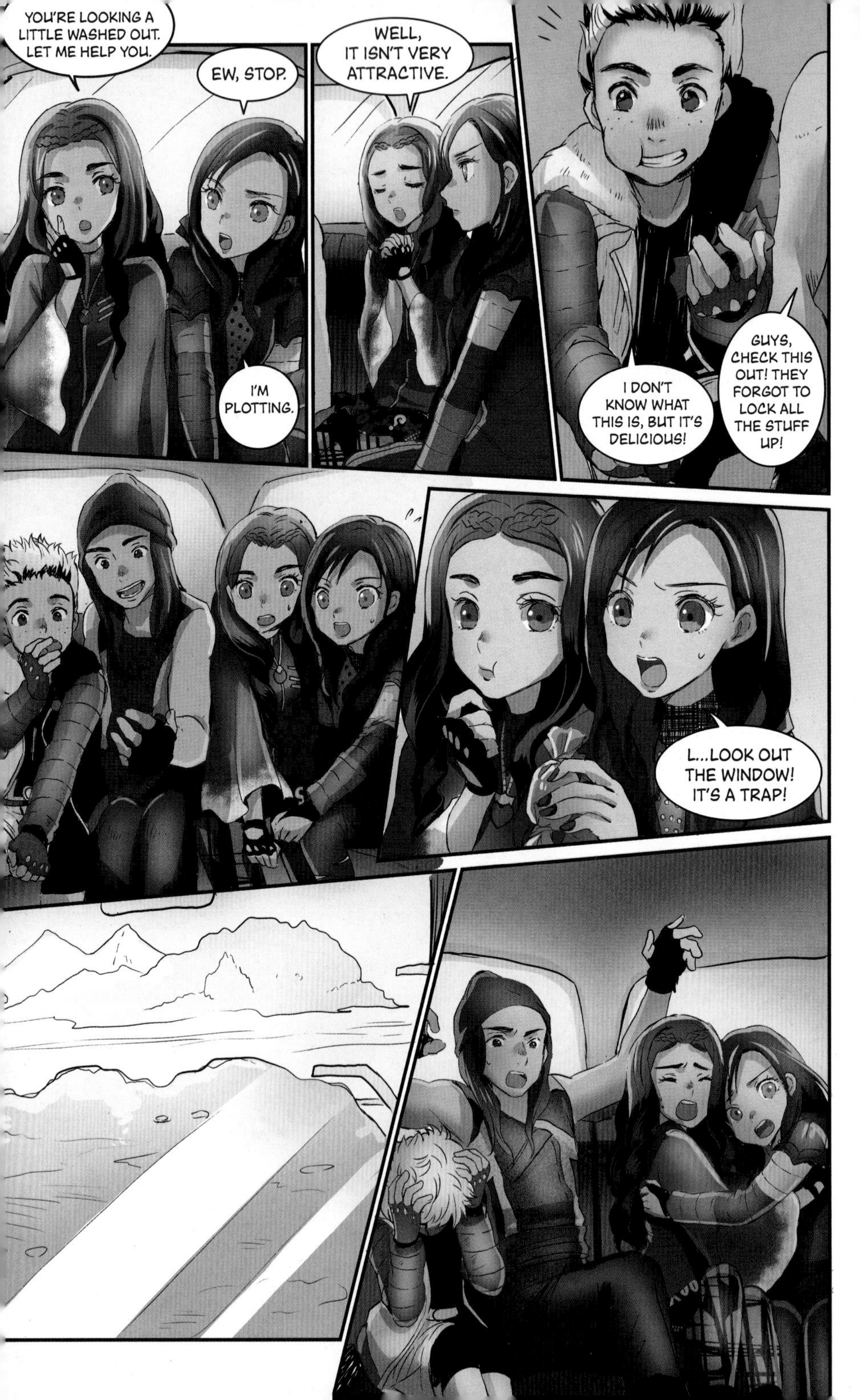
YOU'RE LOOKING A LITTLE WASHED OUT. LET ME HELP YOU.
EW, STOP.
I'M PLOTTING.
WELL, IT ISN'T VERY ATTRACTIVE.
I DON'T KNOW WHAT THIS IS, BUT IT'S DELICIOUS!
GUYS, CHECK THIS OUT! THEY FORGOT TO LOCK ALL THE STUFF UP!
L...LOOK OUT THE WINDOW! IT'S A TRAP!

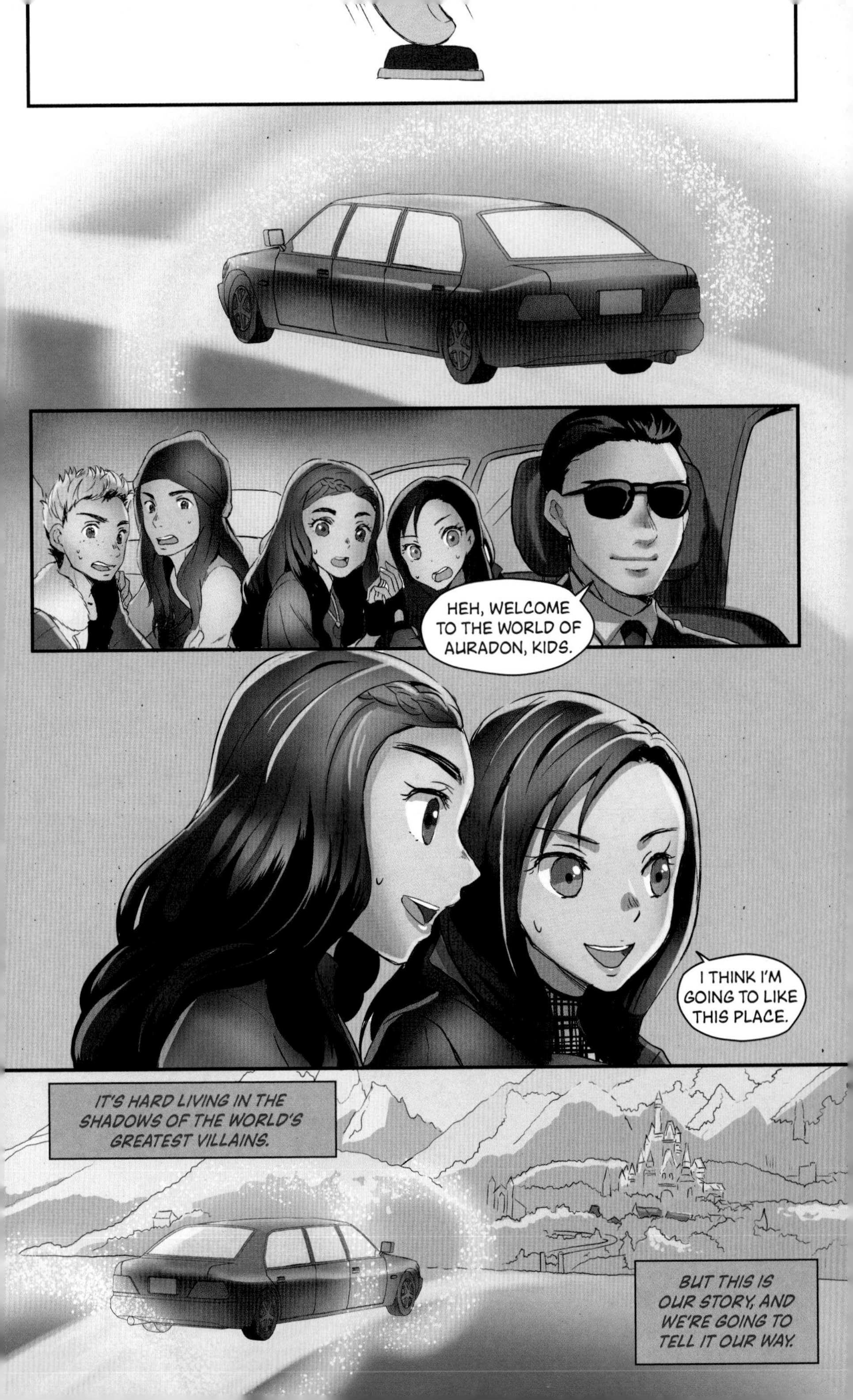
HEH, WELCOME TO THE WORLD OF AURADON, KIDS.
I THINK I'M GOING TO LIKE THIS PLACE.
IT'S HARD LIVING IN THE SHADOWS OF THE WORLD'S GREATEST VILLAINS.
BUT THIS IS OUR STORY, AND WE'RE GOING TO TELL IT OUR WAY.

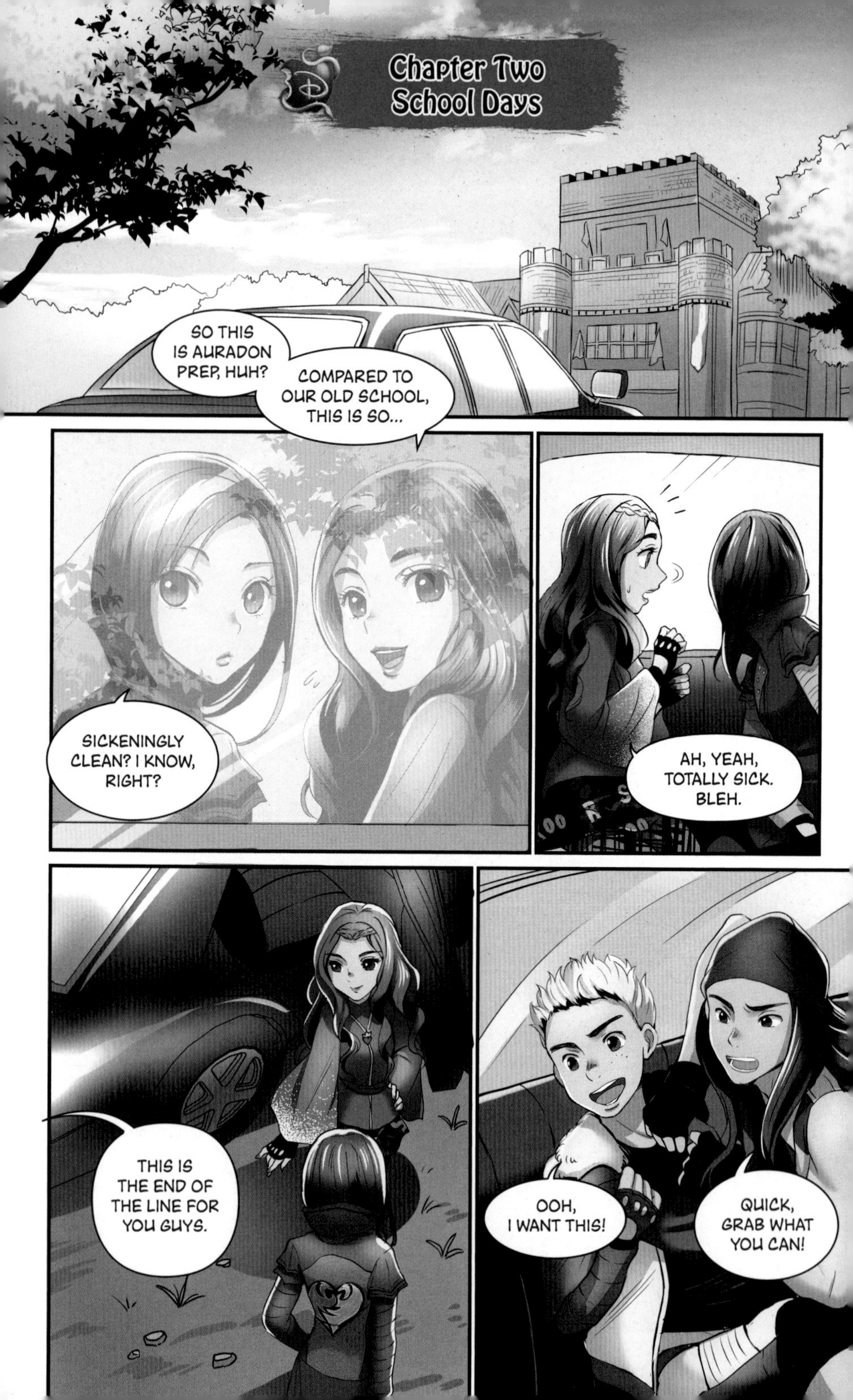
Chapter Two
School Days
SO THIS IS AURADON PREP, HUH?
COMPARED TO OUR OLD SCHOOL, THIS IS SO...
SICKENINGLY CLEAN? I KNOW, RIGHT?
AH, YEAH, TOTALLY SICK. BLEH.
THIS IS THE END OF THE LINE FOR YOU GUYS.
OOH, I WANT THIS!
QUICK, GRAB WHAT YOU CAN!

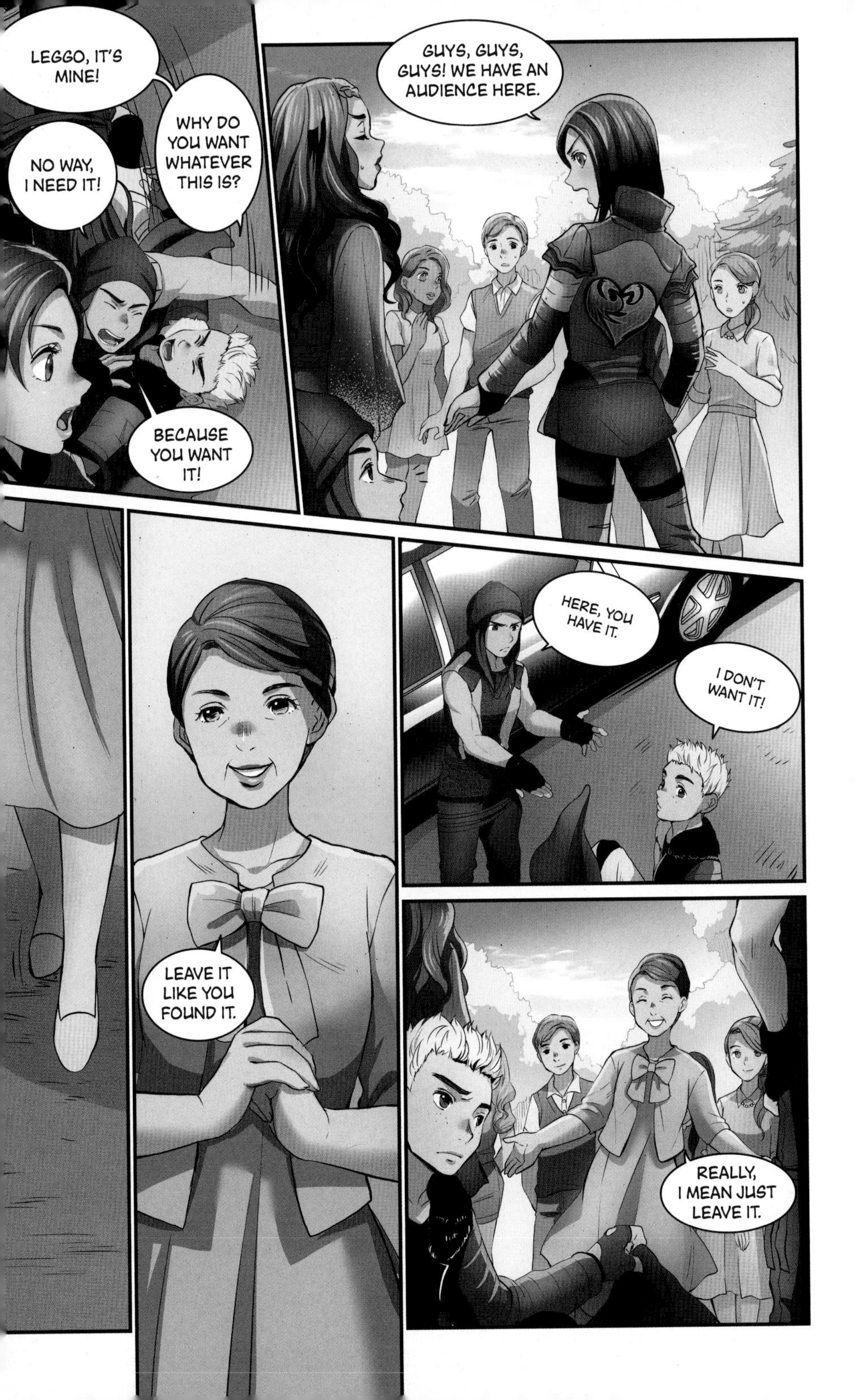
LEGGO, IT'S MINE!
NO WAY, I NEED IT!
WHY DO YOU WANT WHATEVER THIS IS?
BECAUSE YOU WANT IT!
GUYS, GUYS, GUYS! WE HAVE AN AUDIENCE HERE.
LEAVE IT LIKE YOU FOUND IT.
HERE, YOU HAVE IT.
I DON'T WANT IT!
REALLY, I MEAN JUST LEAVE IT.

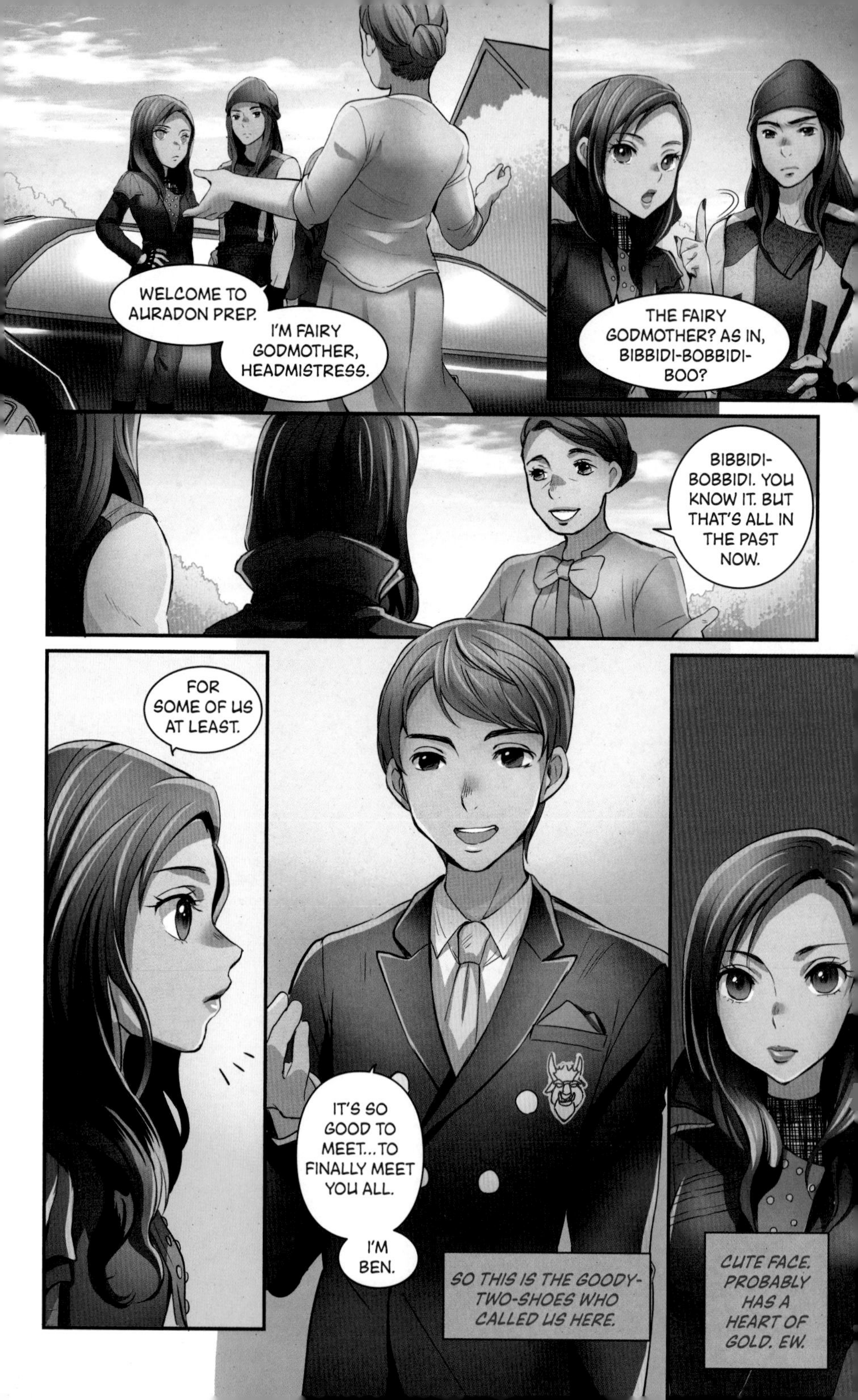
WELCOME TO AURADON PREP.
I'M FAIRY GODMOTHER, HEADMISTRESS.
THE FAIRY GODMOTHER? AS IN, BIBBIDI-BOBBIDI-BOO?
BIBBIDI-BOBBIDI. YOU KNOW IT. BUT THAT'S ALL IN THE PAST NOW.
FOR SOME OF US AT LEAST.
IT'S SO GOOD TO MEET...TO FINALLY MEET YOU ALL.
I'M BEN.
SO THIS IS THE GOODY-TWO-SHOES WHO CALLED US HERE.
CUTE FACE. PROBABLY HAS A HEART OF GOLD. EW.

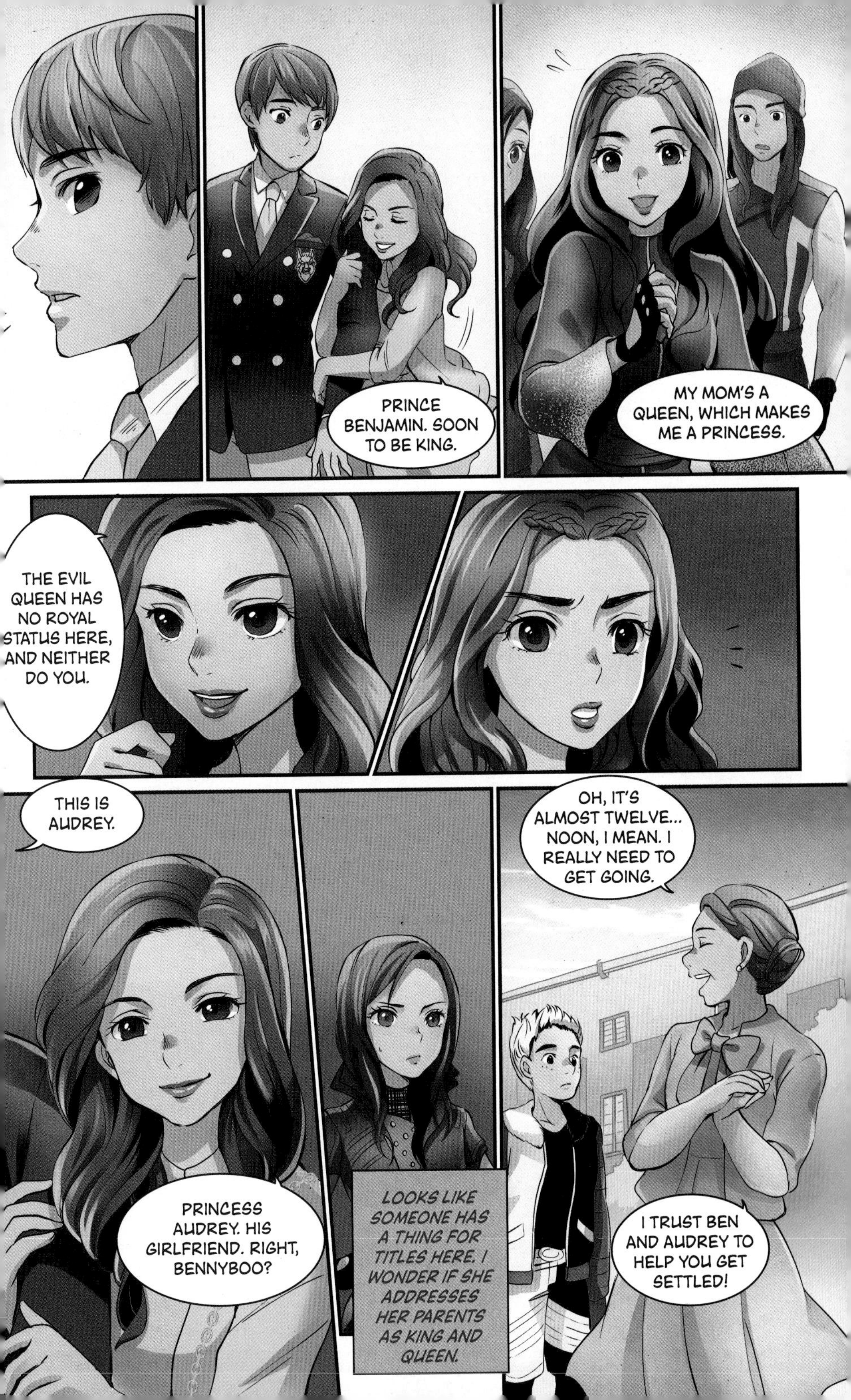
PRINCE BENJAMIN. SOON TO BE KING.
MY MOM'S A QUEEN, WHICH MAKES ME A PRINCESS.
THE EVIL QUEEN HAS NO ROYAL STATUS HERE, AND NEITHER DO YOU.
THIS IS AUDREY.
PRINCESS AUDREY. HIS GIRLFRIEND. RIGHT, BENNYBOO?
LOOKS LIKE SOMEONE HAS A THING FOR TITLES HERE. I WONDER IF SHE ADDRESSES HER PARENTS AS KING AND QUEEN.
OH, IT'S ALMOST TWELVE... NOON, I MEAN. I REALLY NEED TO GET GOING.
I TRUST BEN AND AUDREY TO HELP YOU GET SETTLED!

IT IS SO, SO, SO GOOD TO FINALLY MEET YOU ALL.

THIS IS A DAY THAT I HOPE WILL GO DOWN IN HISTORY AS...

WHO WROTE THIS SPEECH?

THE DAY THAT YOU SHOWED FOUR PEOPLE WHERE THE BATHROOMS ARE?

A LITTLE BIT OVER THE TOP

A LITTLE MORE THAN A LITTLE BIT.

SO MUCH FOR FIRST IMPRESSIONS. I GUESS WE SHOULD GET YOU ON YOUR WAY.

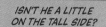

DOUG, COME DOWN. THIS IS DOUG, HE'LL BE ABLE TO ANSWER ANY QUESTION YOU HAVE.

HI, GUYS. I'M DOPEY'S SON. AS IN DOPEY, DOC, BASHFUL...

ISN'T HE A LITTLE ON THE TALL SIDE?

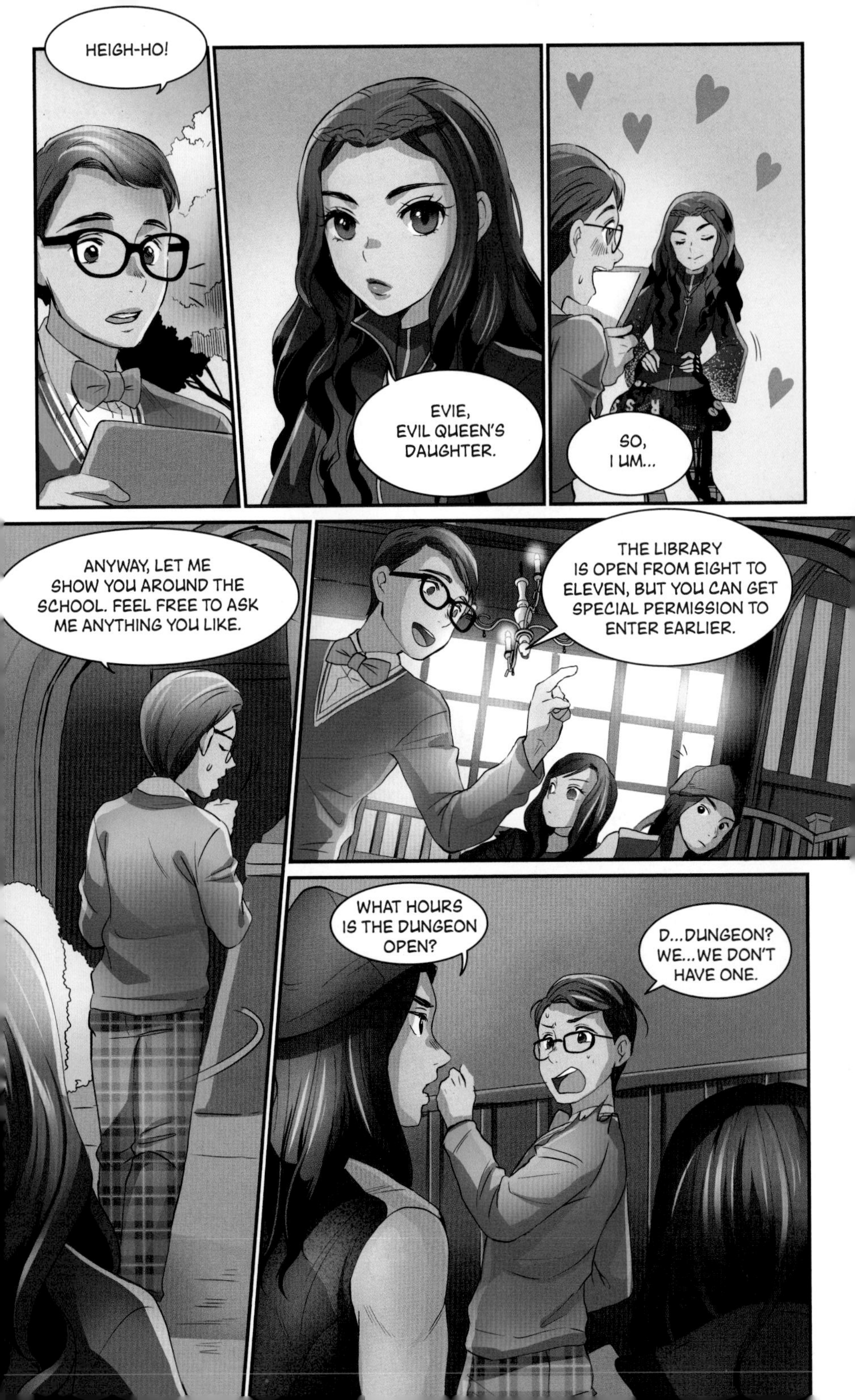
HEIGH-HO!
EVIE, EVIL QUEEN'S DAUGHTER.
SO, I UM...
ANYWAY, LET ME SHOW YOU AROUND THE SCHOOL. FEEL FREE TO ASK ME ANYTHING YOU LIKE.
THE LIBRARY IS OPEN FROM EIGHT TO ELEVEN, BUT YOU CAN GET SPECIAL PERMISSION TO ENTER EARLIER.
WHAT HOURS IS THE DUNGEON OPEN?
D...DUNGEON? WE...WE DON'T HAVE ONE.

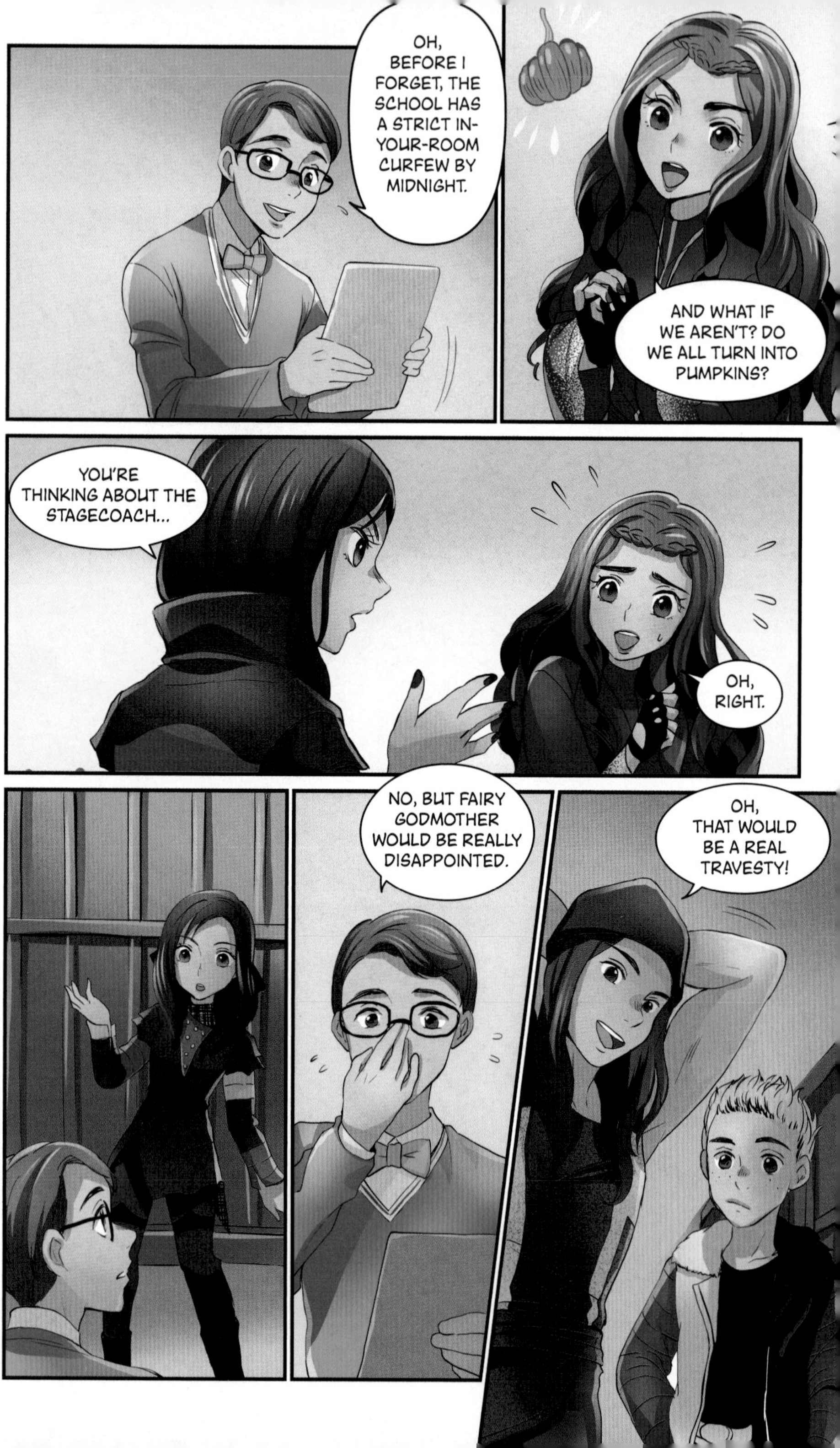
OH, BEFORE I FORGET, THE SCHOOL HAS A STRICT IN-YOUR-ROOM CURFEW BY MIDNIGHT.
AND WHAT IF WE AREN'T? DO WE ALL TURN INTO PUMPKINS?
YOU'RE THINKING ABOUT THE STAGECOACH...
OH, RIGHT.
NO, BUT FAIRY GODMOTHER WOULD BE REALLY DISAPPOINTED.
OH, THAT WOULD BE A REAL TRAVESTY!

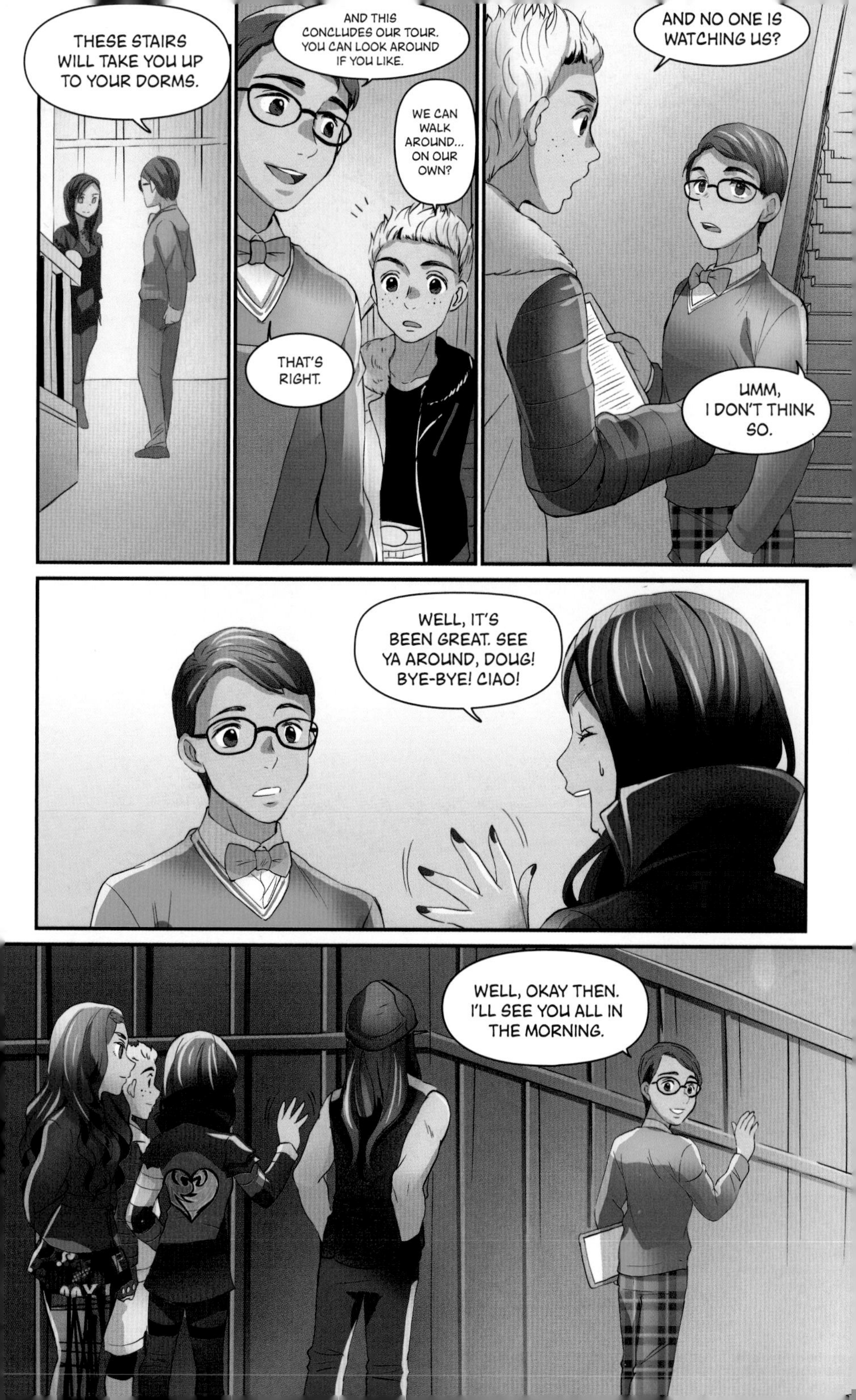
THESE STAIRS WILL TAKE YOU UP TO YOUR DORMS.
AND THIS CONCLUDES OUR TOUR. YOU CAN LOOK AROUND IF YOU LIKE.
WE CAN WALK AROUND... ON OUR OWN?
THAT'S RIGHT.
AND NO ONE IS WATCHING US?
UMM, I DON'T THINK SO.
WELL, IT'S BEEN GREAT. SEE YA AROUND, DOUG! BYE-BYE! CIAO!
WELL, OKAY THEN. I'LL SEE YOU ALL IN THE MORNING.

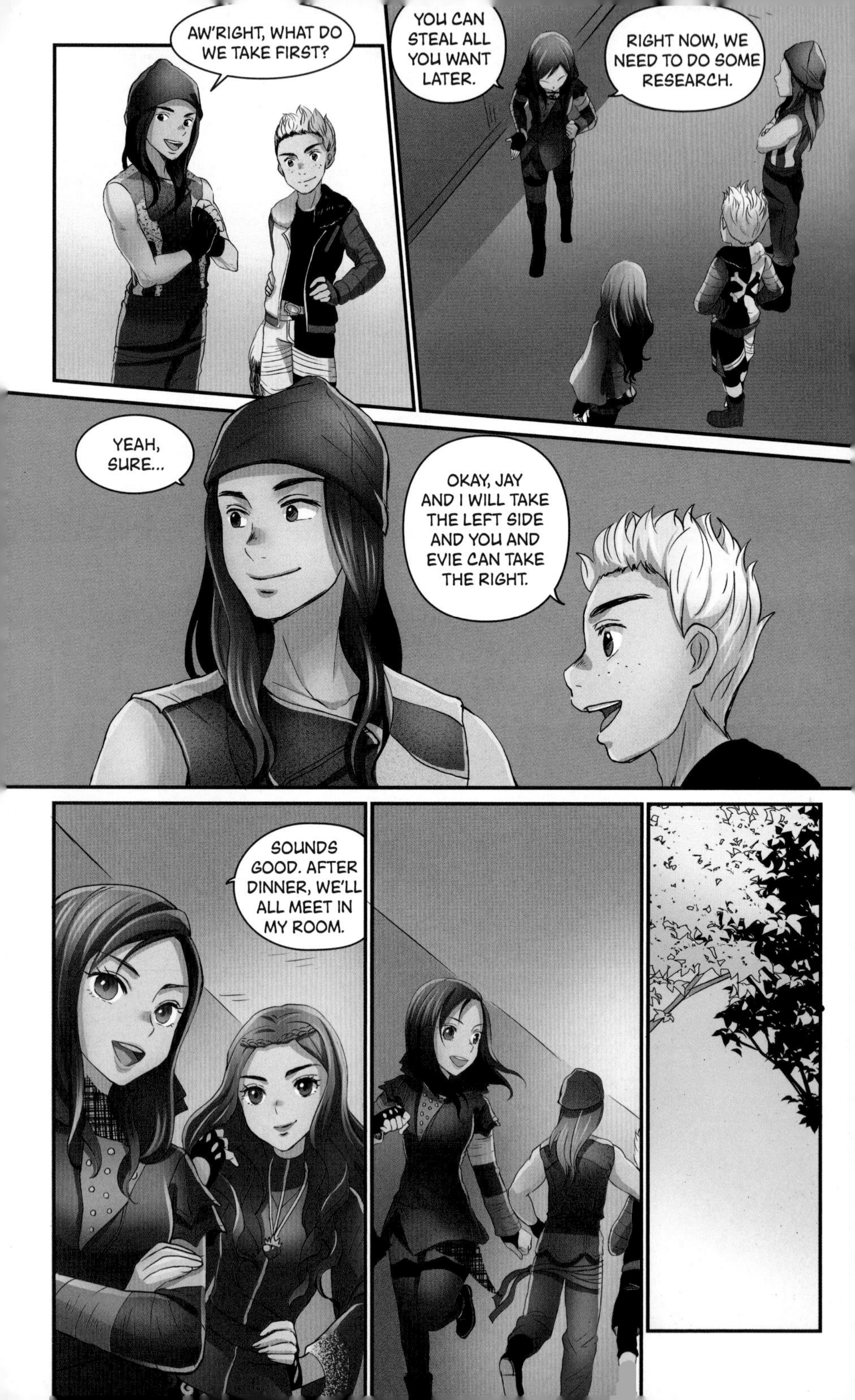
AW'RIGHT, WHAT DO WE TAKE FIRST?
YOU CAN STEAL ALL YOU WANT LATER.
RIGHT NOW, WE NEED TO DO SOME RESEARCH.
YEAH, SURE...
OKAY, JAY AND I WILL TAKE THE LEFT SIDE AND YOU AND EVIE CAN TAKE THE RIGHT.
SOUNDS GOOD. AFTER DINNER, WE'LL ALL MEET IN MY ROOM.

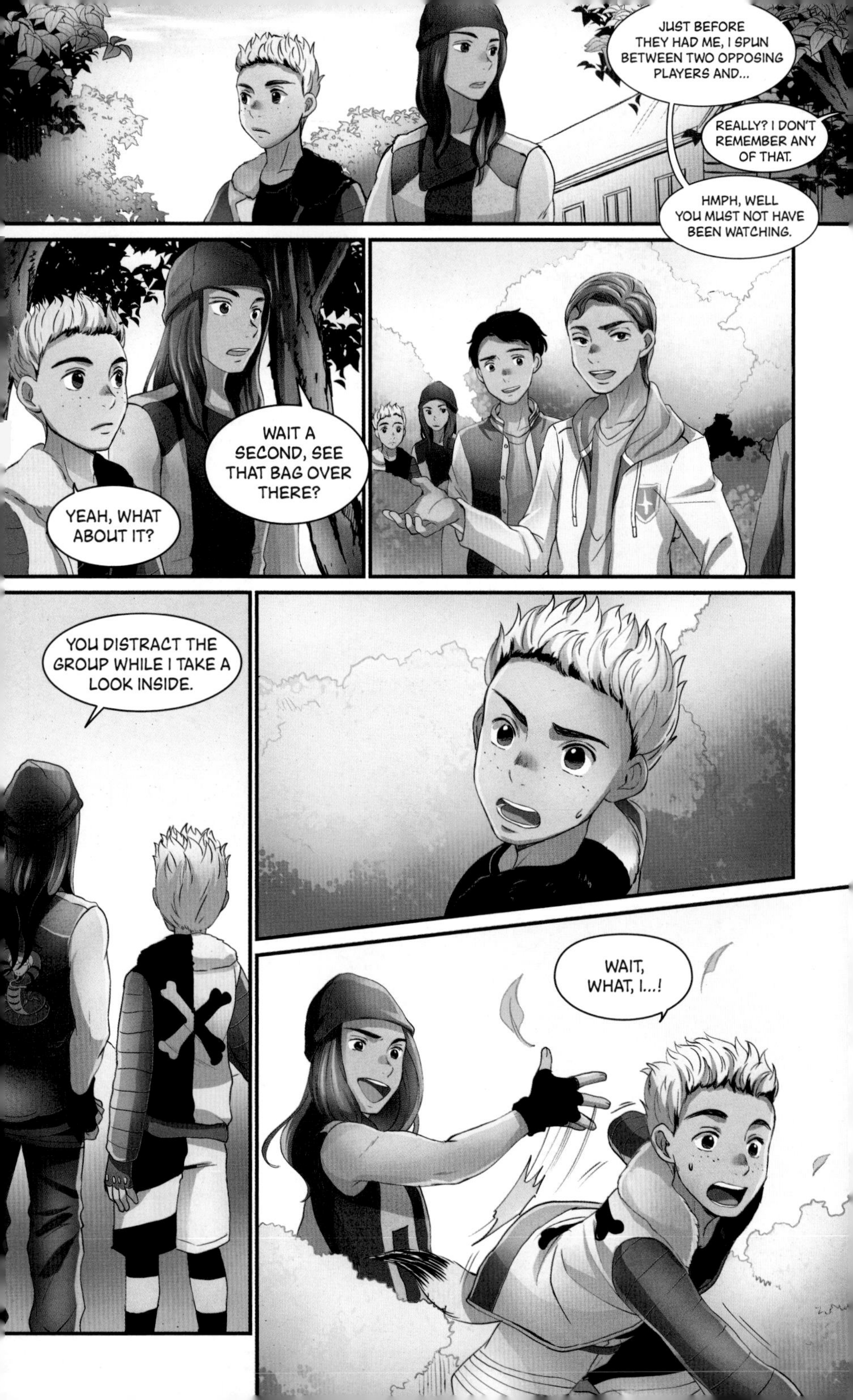
JUST BEFORE THEY HAD ME, I SPUN BETWEEN TWO OPPOSING PLAYERS AND...
REALLY? I DON'T REMEMBER ANY OF THAT.
HMPH, WELL YOU MUST NOT HAVE BEEN WATCHING.
WAIT A SECOND, SEE THAT BAG OVER THERE?
YEAH, WHAT ABOUT IT?
YOU DISTRACT THE GROUP WHILE I TAKE A LOOK INSIDE.
WAIT, WHAT, I...!

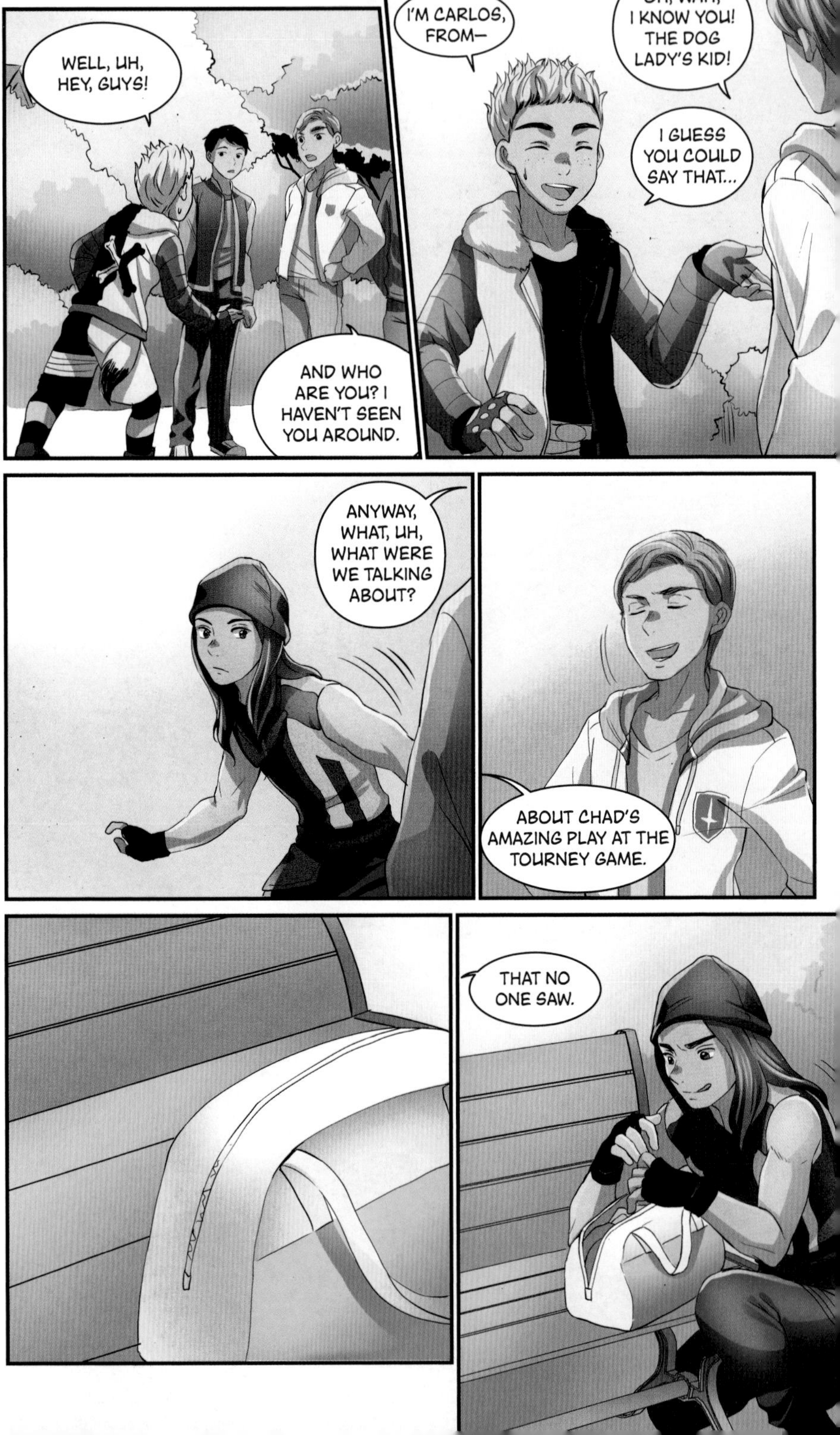
WELL, UH, HEY, GUYS!
AND WHO ARE YOU? I HAVEN'T SEEN YOU AROUND.
I'M CARLOS, FROM—
OH, WAIT, I KNOW YOU! THE DOG LADY'S KID!
I GUESS YOU COULD SAY THAT...
ANYWAY, WHAT, UH, WHAT WERE WE TALKING ABOUT?
ABOUT CHAD'S AMAZING PLAY AT THE TOURNEY GAME.
THAT NO ONE SAW.

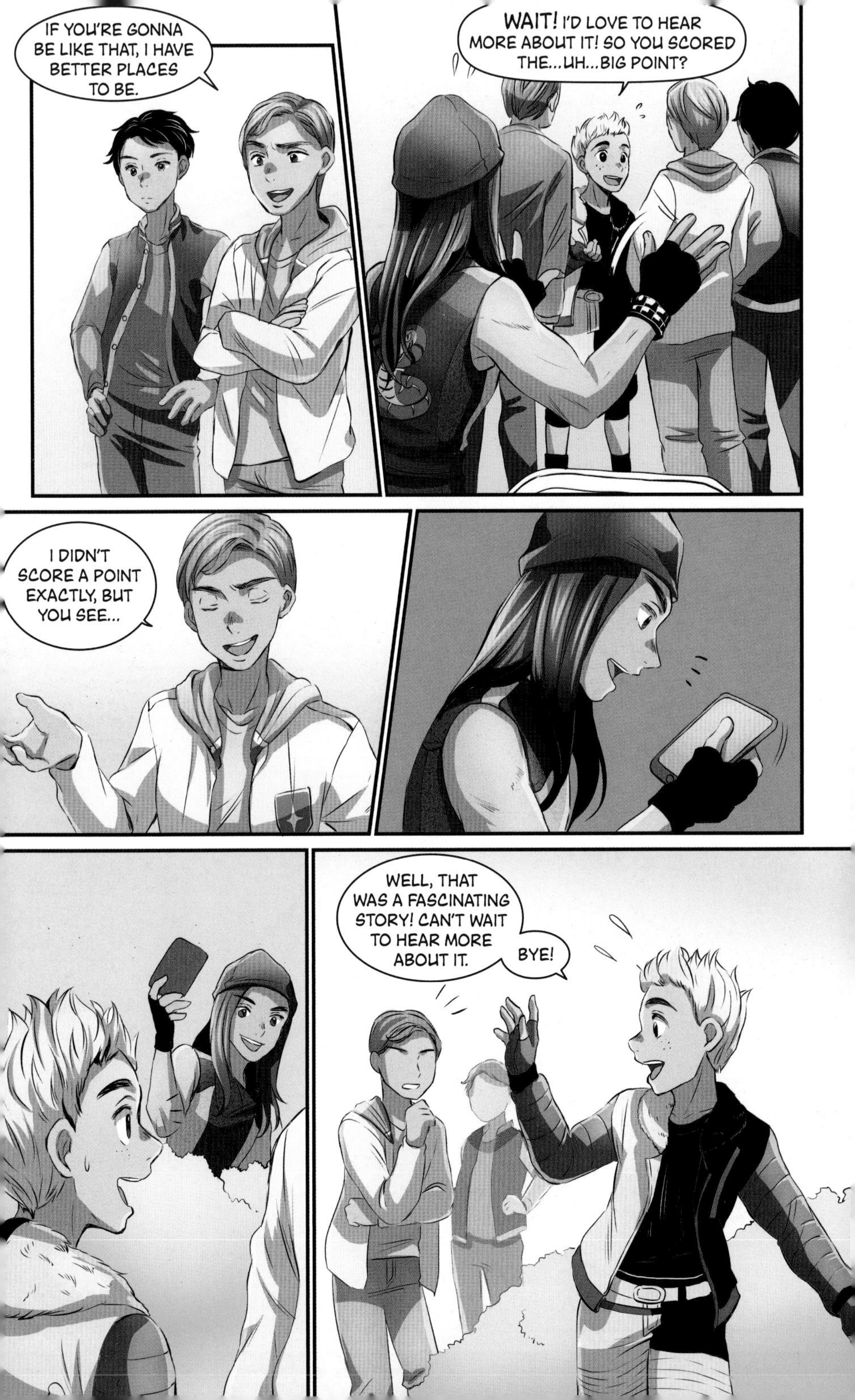
IF YOU'RE GONNA BE LIKE THAT, I HAVE BETTER PLACES TO BE.
WAIT! I'D LOVE TO HEAR MORE ABOUT IT! SO YOU SCORED THE...UH...BIG POINT?
I DIDN'T SCORE A POINT EXACTLY, BUT YOU SEE...
WELL, THAT WAS A FASCINATING STORY! CAN'T WAIT TO HEAR MORE ABOUT IT.
BYE!

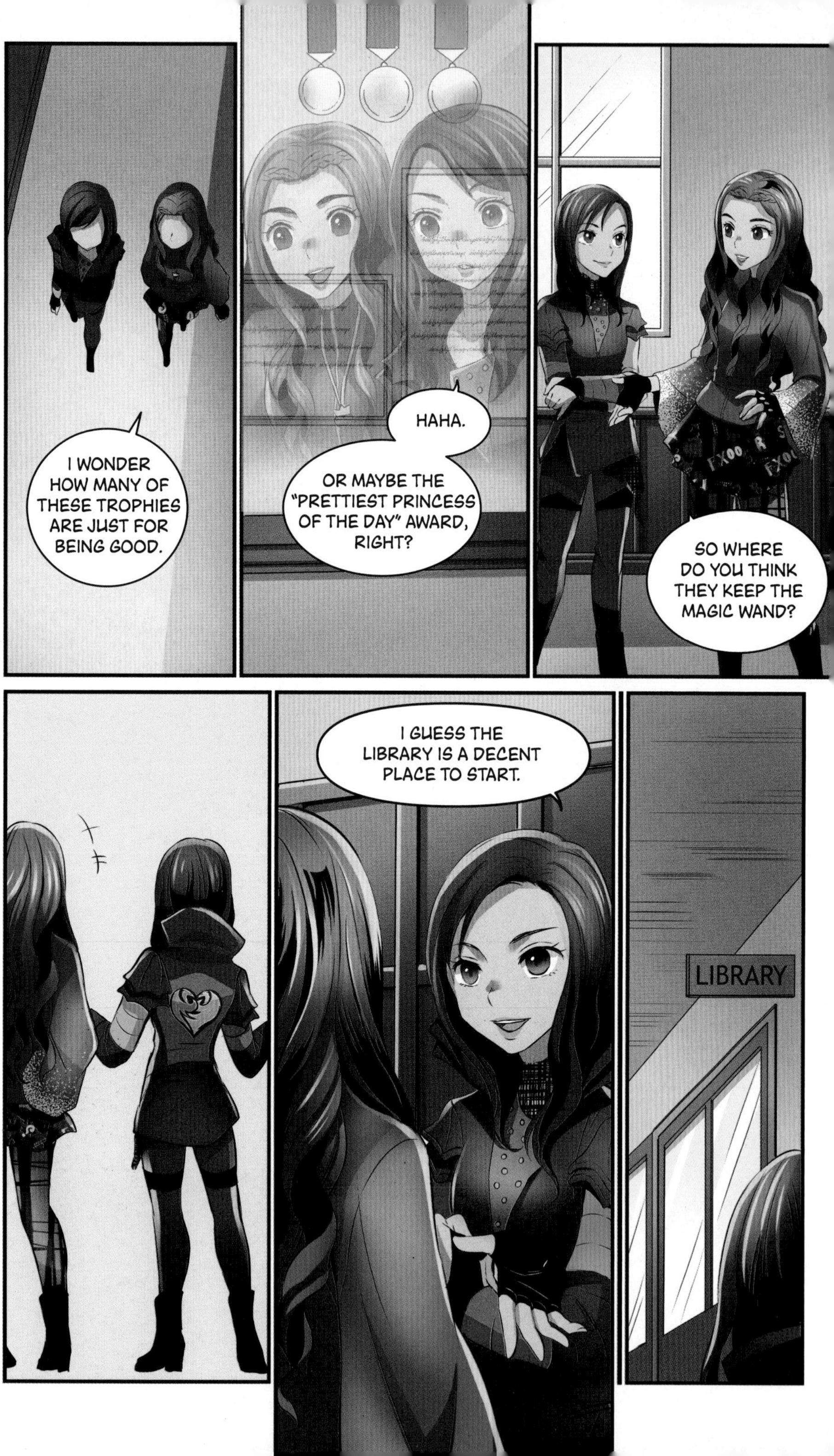
I WONDER HOW MANY OF THESE TROPHIES ARE JUST FOR BEING GOOD.
HAHA.
OR MAYBE THE "PRETTIEST PRINCESS OF THE DAY" AWARD, RIGHT?
SO WHERE DO YOU THINK THEY KEEP THE MAGIC WAND?
I GUESS THE LIBRARY IS A DECENT PLACE TO START.
LIBRARY

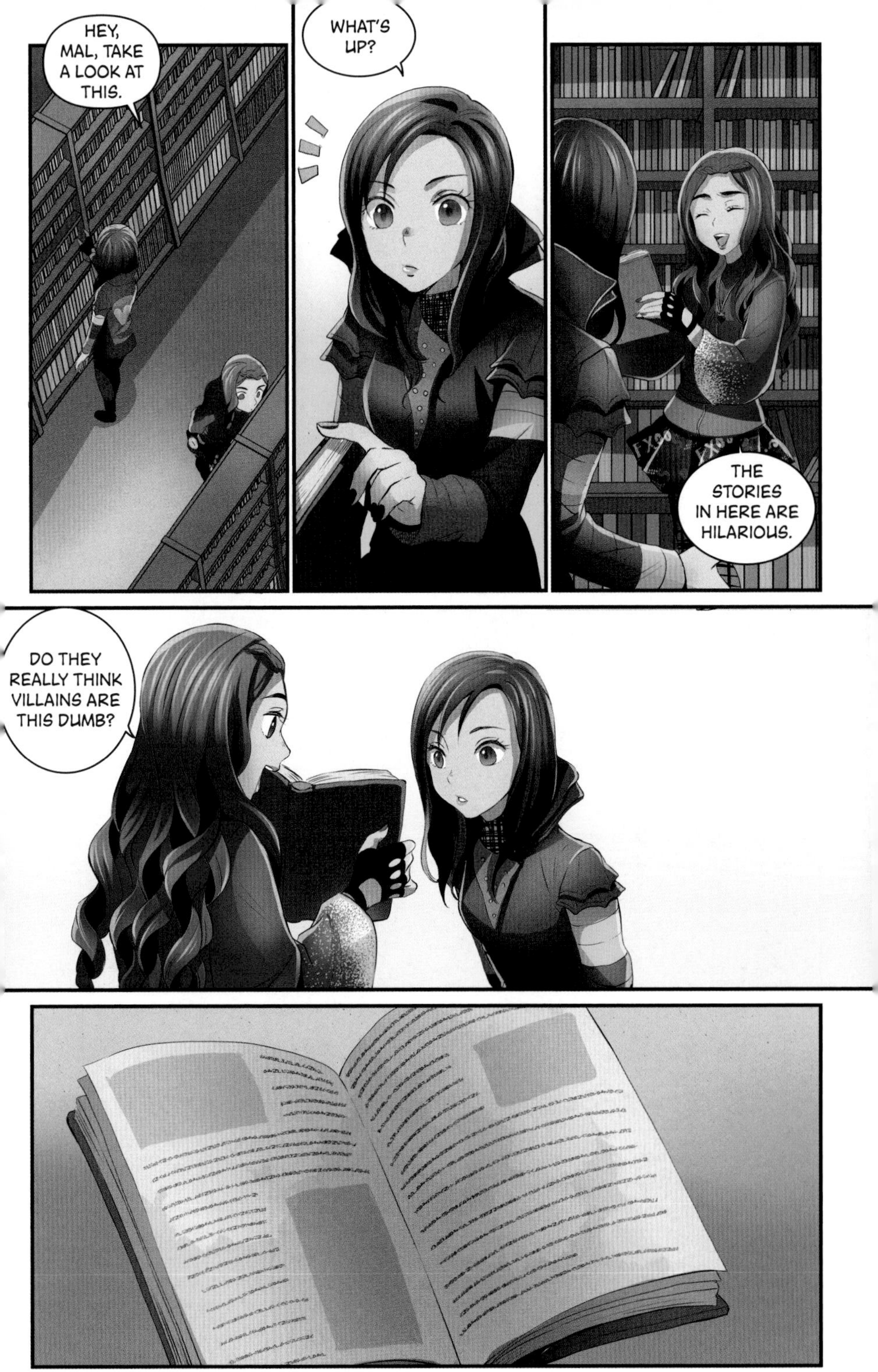
HEY, MAL, TAKE A LOOK AT THIS.
WHAT'S UP?
THE STORIES IN HERE ARE HILARIOUS.
DO THEY REALLY THINK VILLAINS ARE THIS DUMB?

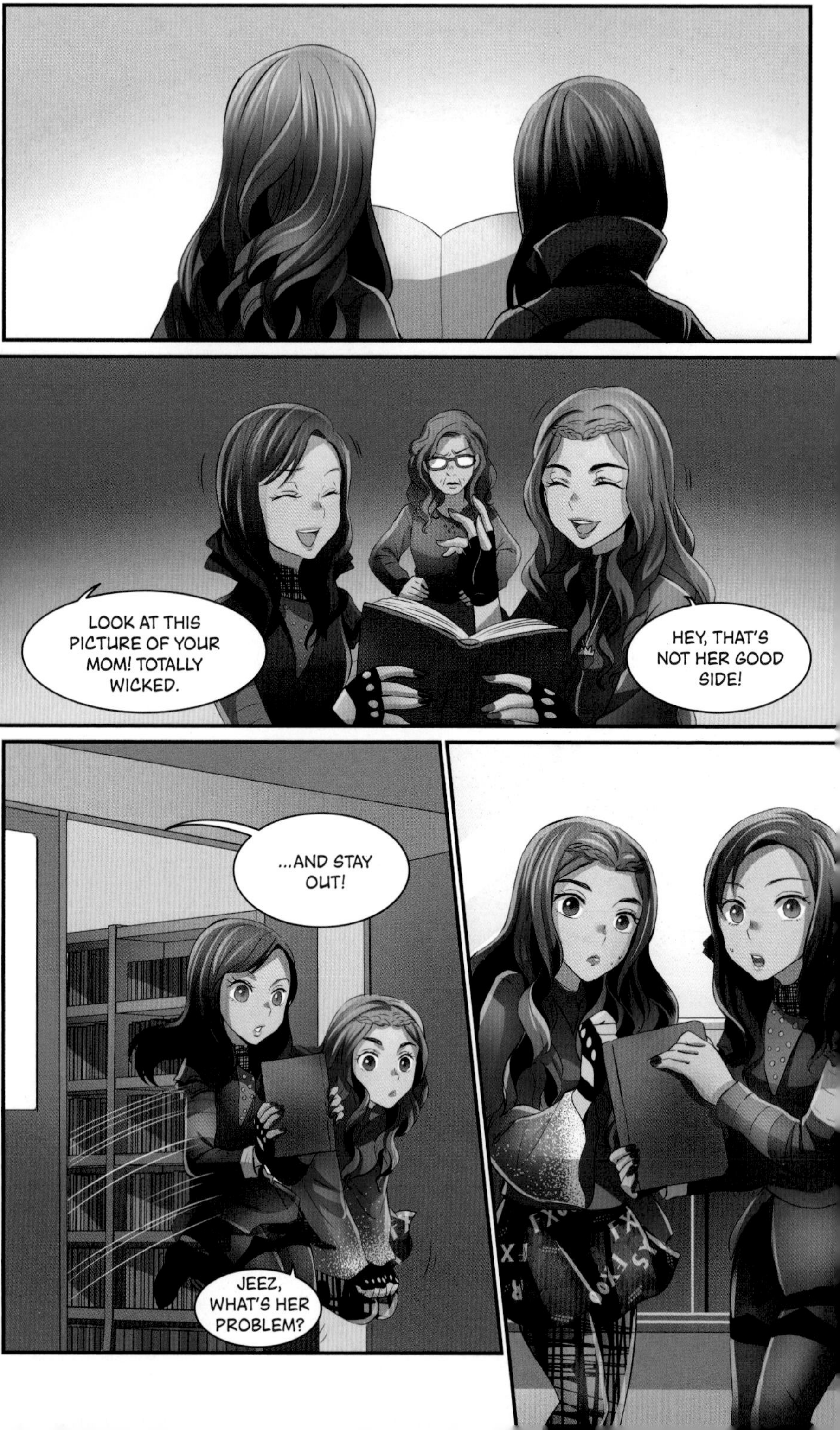
LOOK AT THIS PICTURE OF YOUR MOM! TOTALLY WICKED.
HEY, THAT'S NOT HER GOOD SIDE!
...AND STAY OUT!
JEEZ, WHAT'S HER PROBLEM?

HEY, DID YOU FIND ANYTHING GOOD TO EAT?

UMM... NO?

IS THAT...?

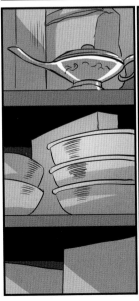

IT'S THE LAMP!

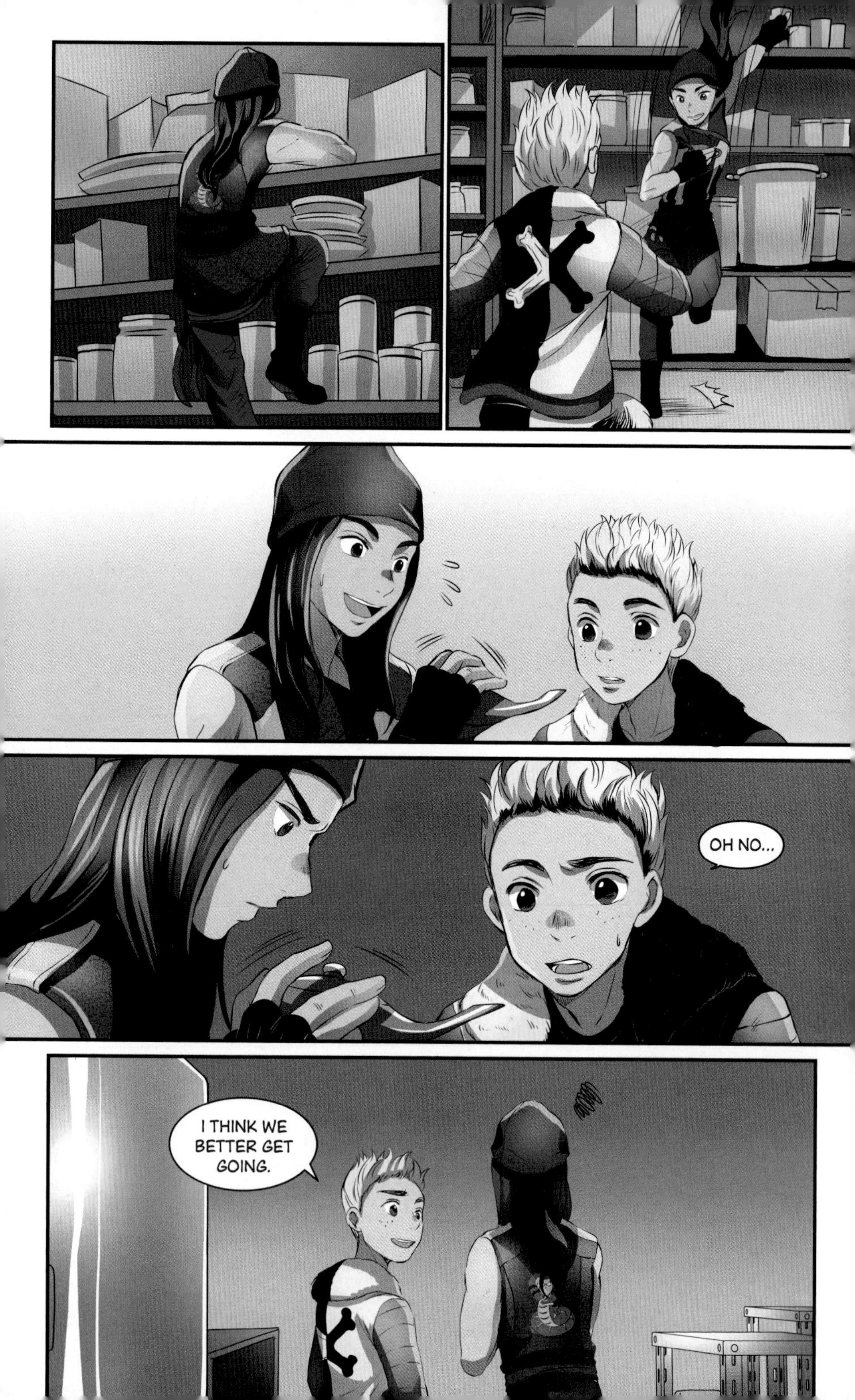
OH NO...
I THINK WE BETTER GET GOING.

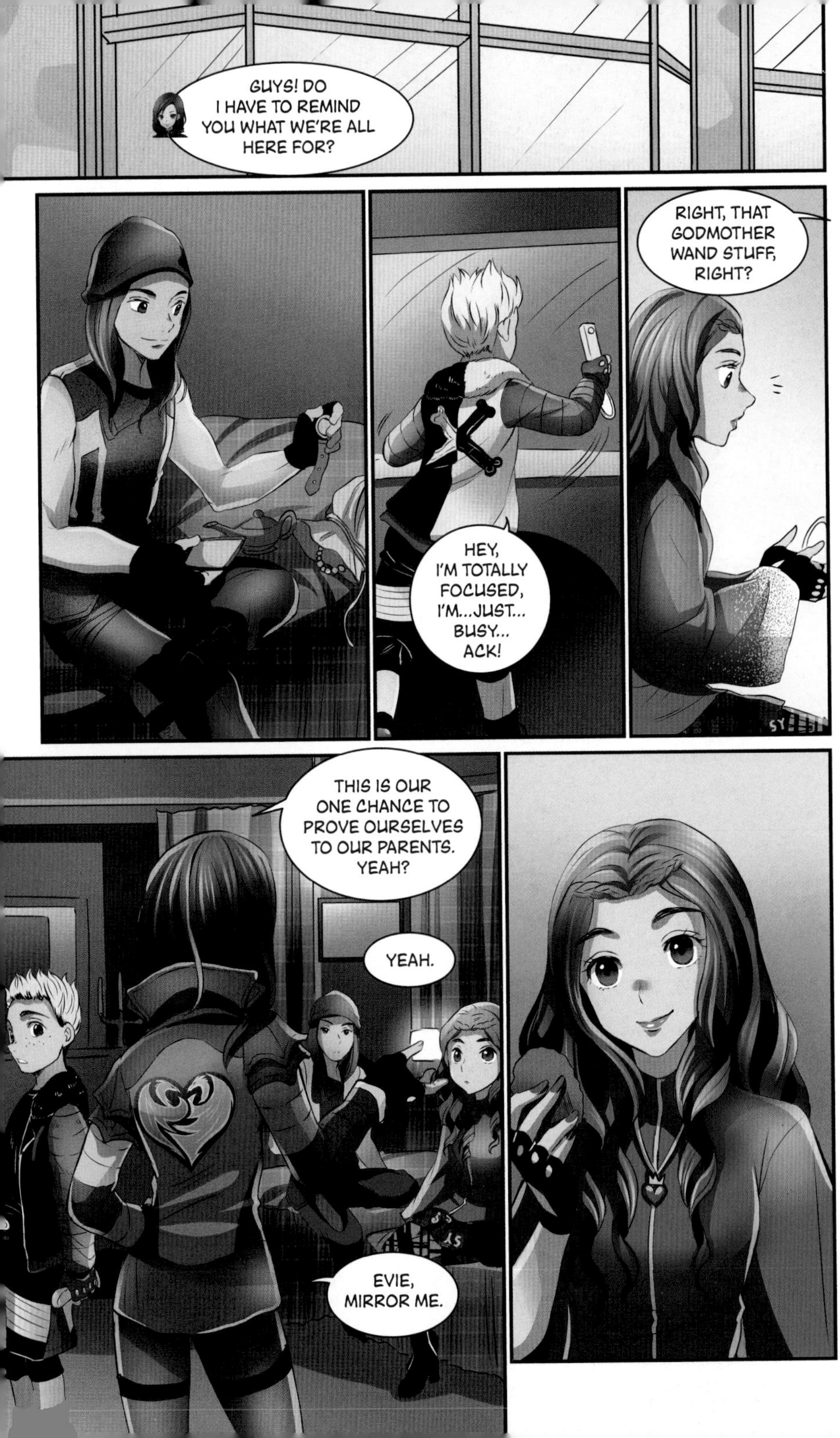
GUYS! DO I HAVE TO REMIND YOU WHAT WE'RE ALL HERE FOR?
HEY, I'M TOTALLY FOCUSED, I'M...JUST... BUSY... ACK!
RIGHT, THAT GODMOTHER WAND STUFF, RIGHT?
THIS IS OUR ONE CHANCE TO PROVE OURSELVES TO OUR PARENTS. YEAH?
YEAH.
EVIE, MIRROR ME.

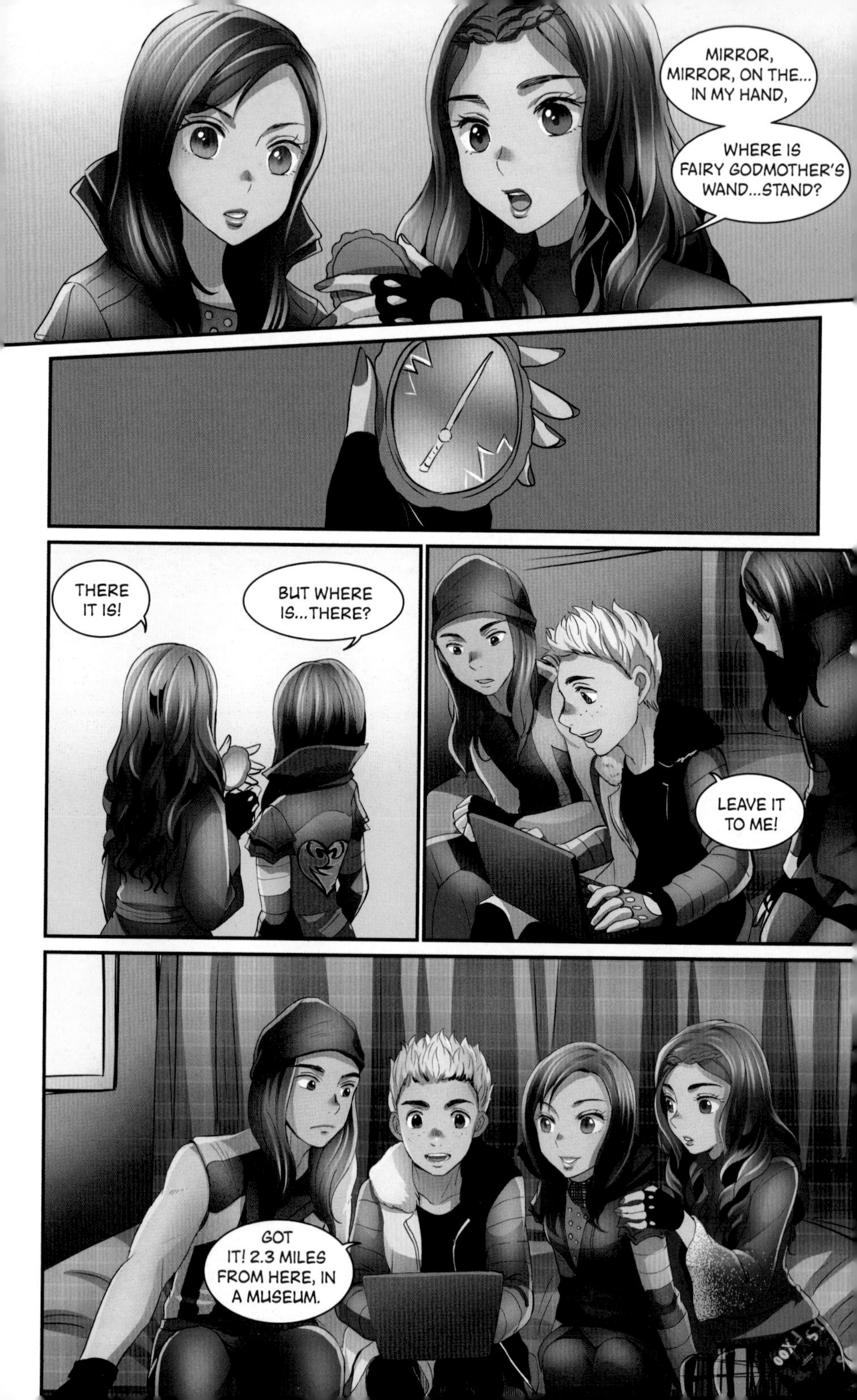
MIRROR, MIRROR, ON THE... IN MY HAND,
WHERE IS FAIRY GODMOTHER'S WAND...STAND?
THERE IT IS!
BUT WHERE IS...THERE?
LEAVE IT TO ME!
GOT IT! 2.3 MILES FROM HERE, IN A MUSEUM.

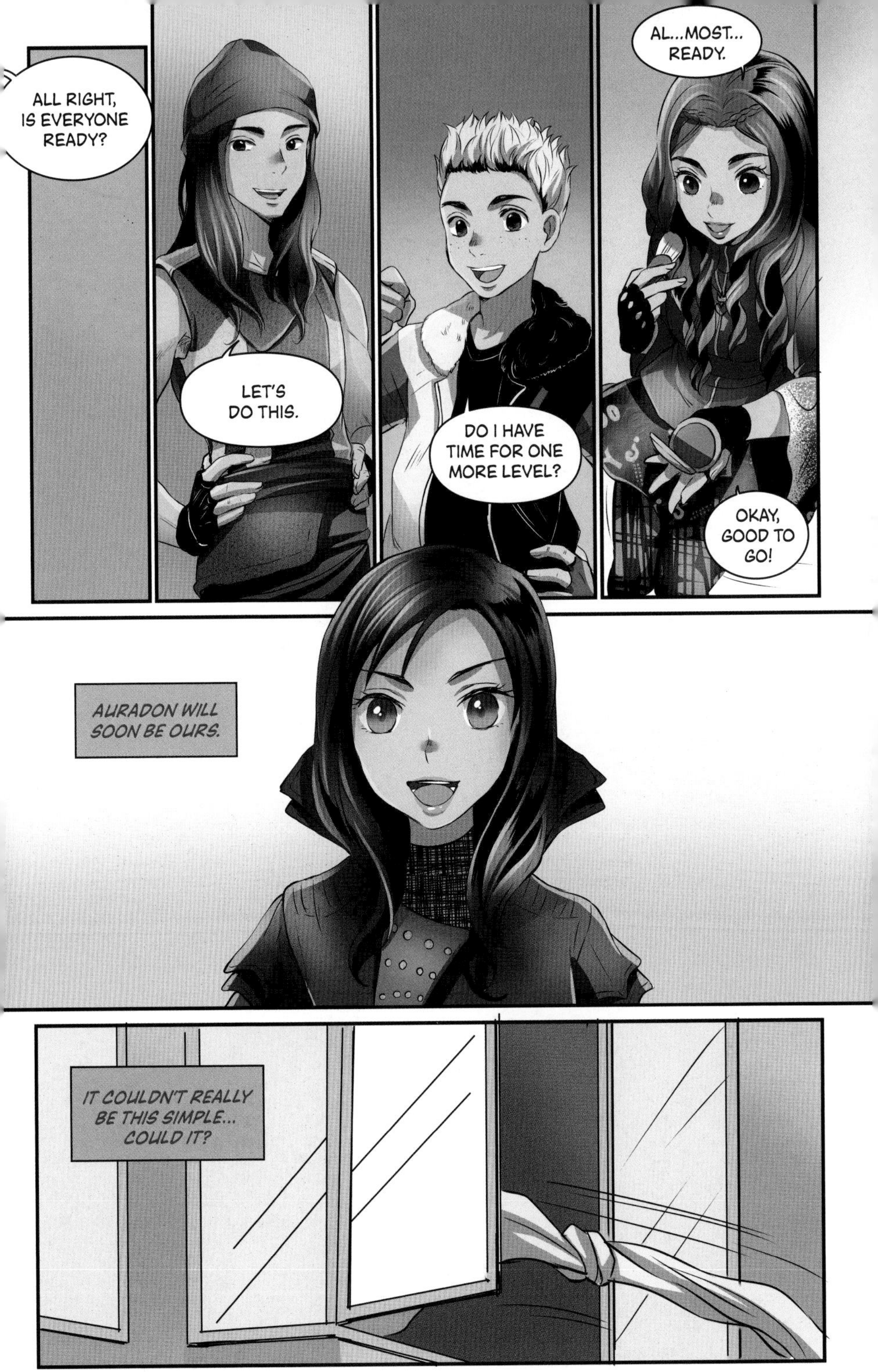
ALL RIGHT, IS EVERYONE READY?
LET'S DO THIS.
DO I HAVE TIME FOR ONE MORE LEVEL?
AL...MOST... READY.
OKAY, GOOD TO GO!
AURADON WILL SOON BE OURS.
IT COULDN'T REALLY BE THIS SIMPLE... COULD IT?

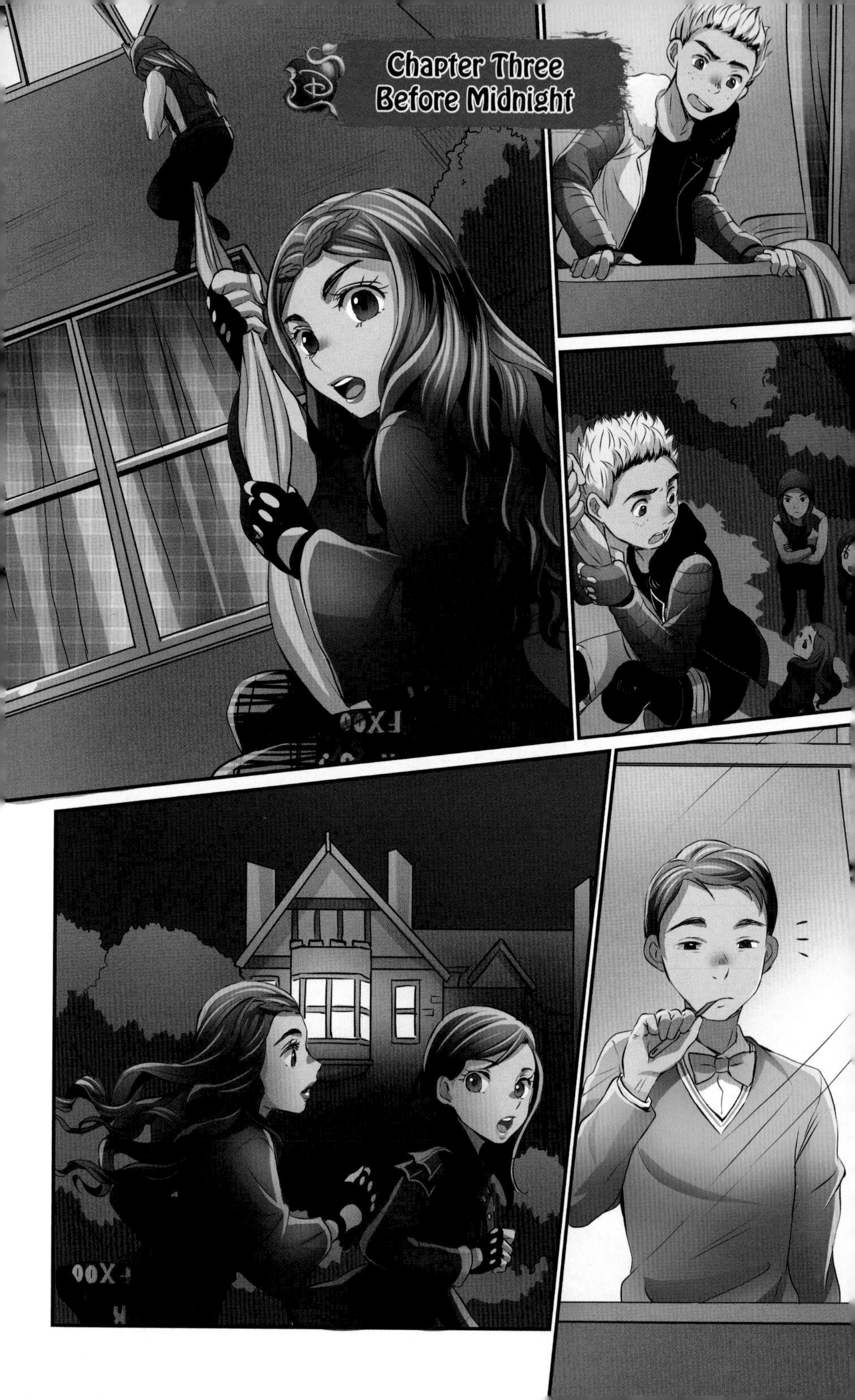
Chapter Three
Before Midnight

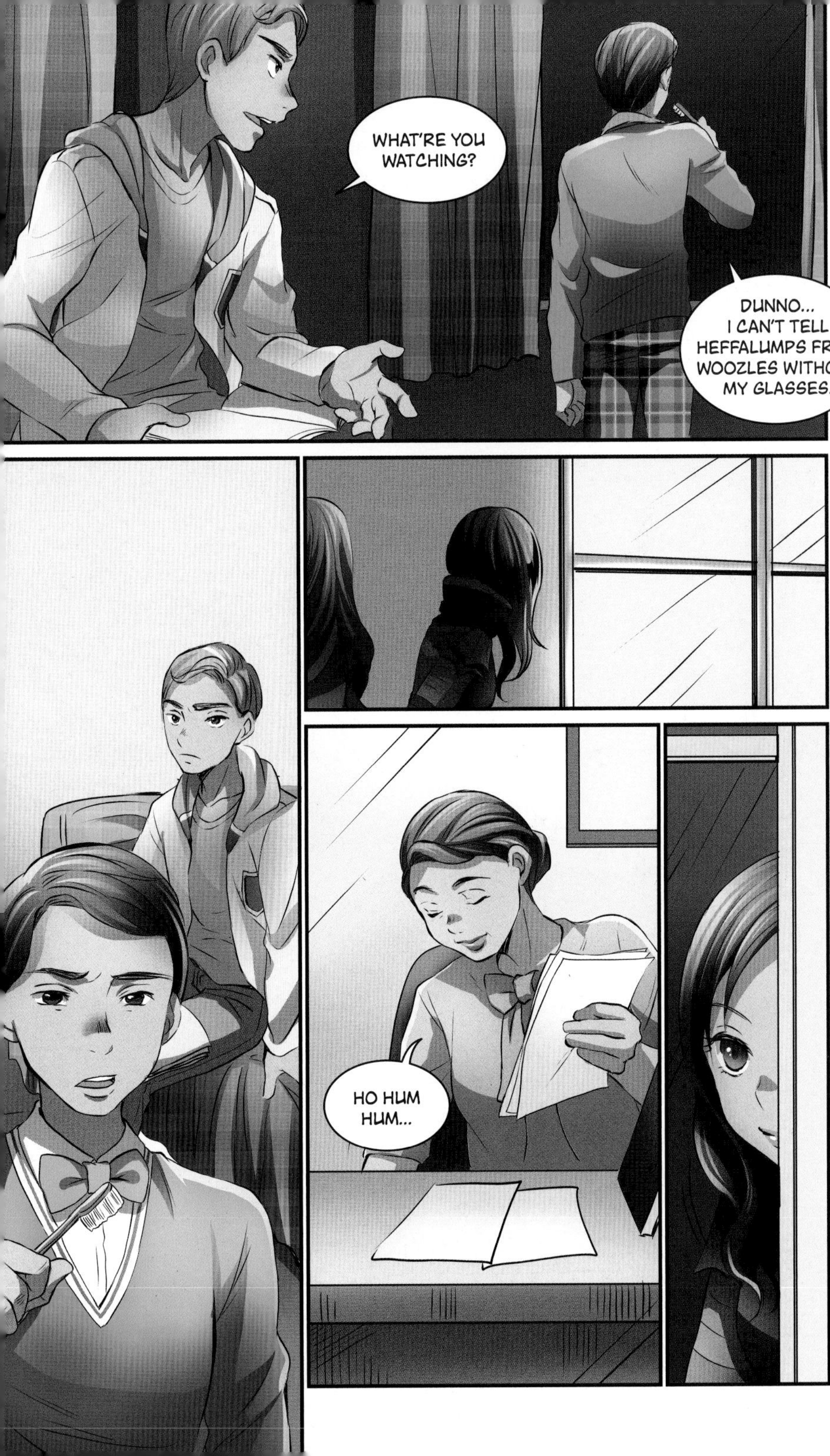
WHAT'RE YOU WATCHING?
DUNNO... I CAN'T TELL HEFFALUMPS FROM WOOZLES WITHOUT MY GLASSES.
HO HUM HUM...

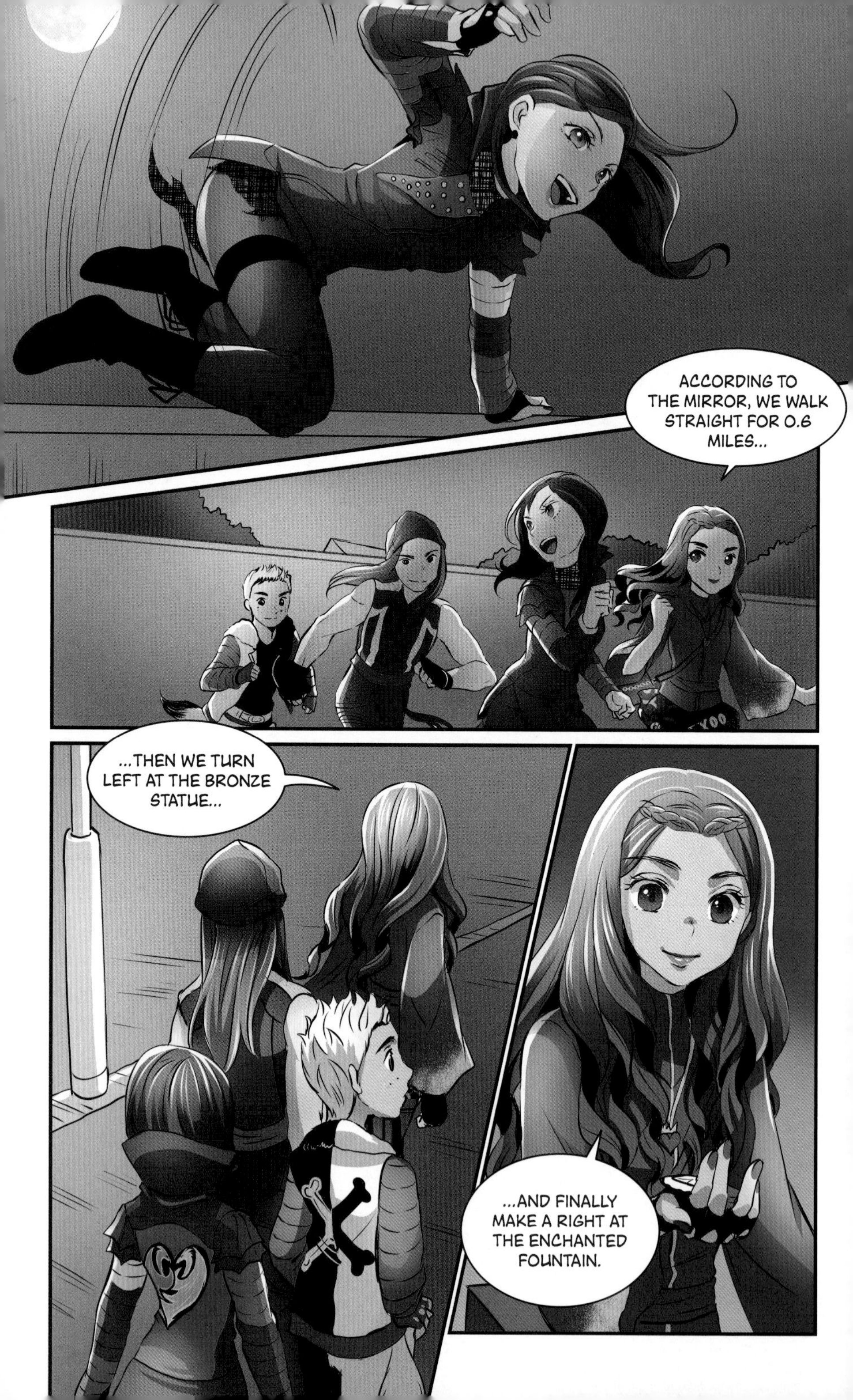
ACCORDING TO THE MIRROR, WE WALK STRAIGHT FOR 0.6 MILES...
...THEN WE TURN LEFT AT THE BRONZE STATUE...
...AND FINALLY MAKE A RIGHT AT THE ENCHANTED FOUNTAIN.

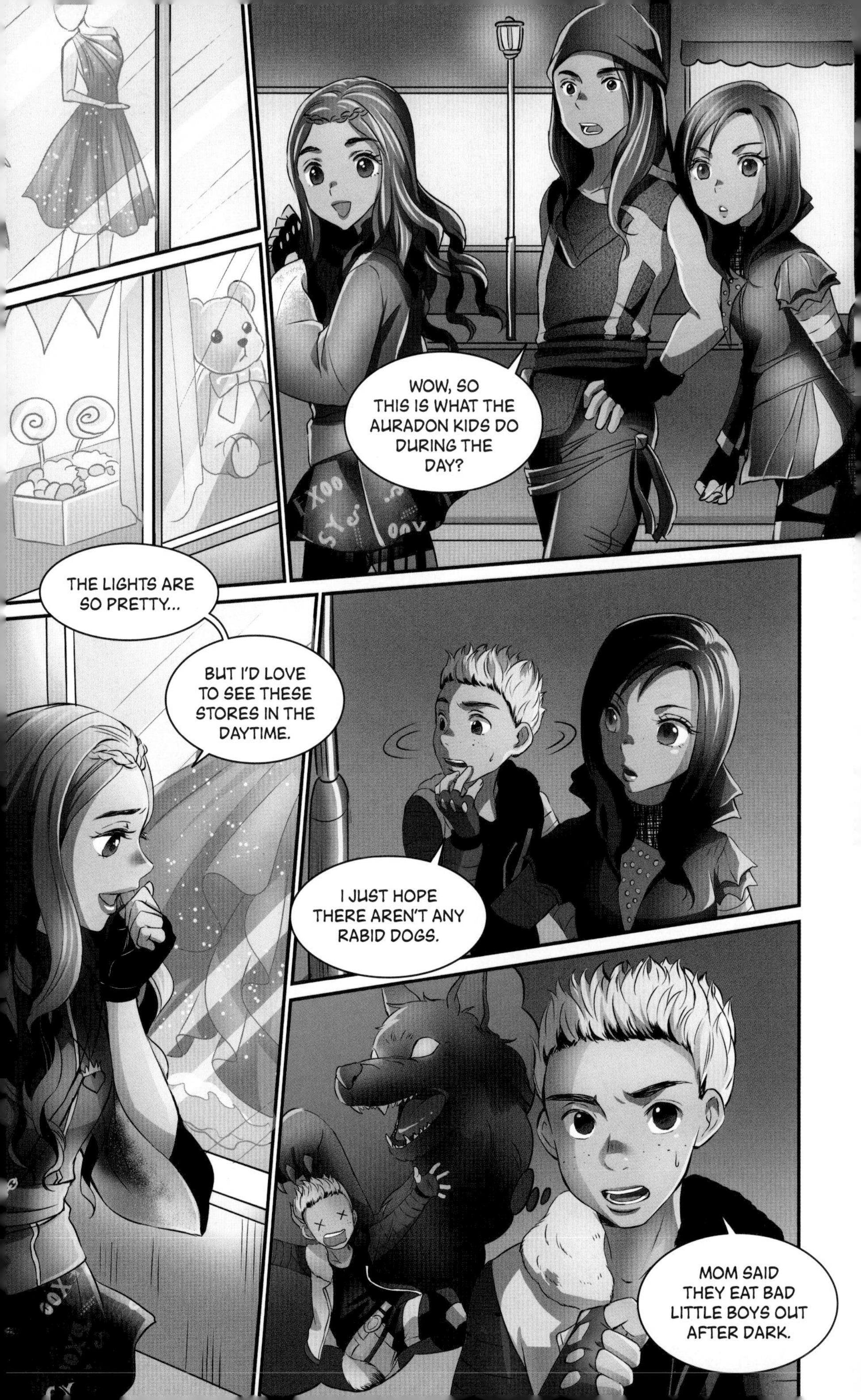
WOW, SO THIS IS WHAT THE AURADON KIDS DO DURING THE DAY?
THE LIGHTS ARE SO PRETTY...
BUT I'D LOVE TO SEE THESE STORES IN THE DAYTIME.
I JUST HOPE THERE AREN'T ANY RABID DOGS.
MOM SAID THEY EAT BAD LITTLE BOYS OUT AFTER DARK.

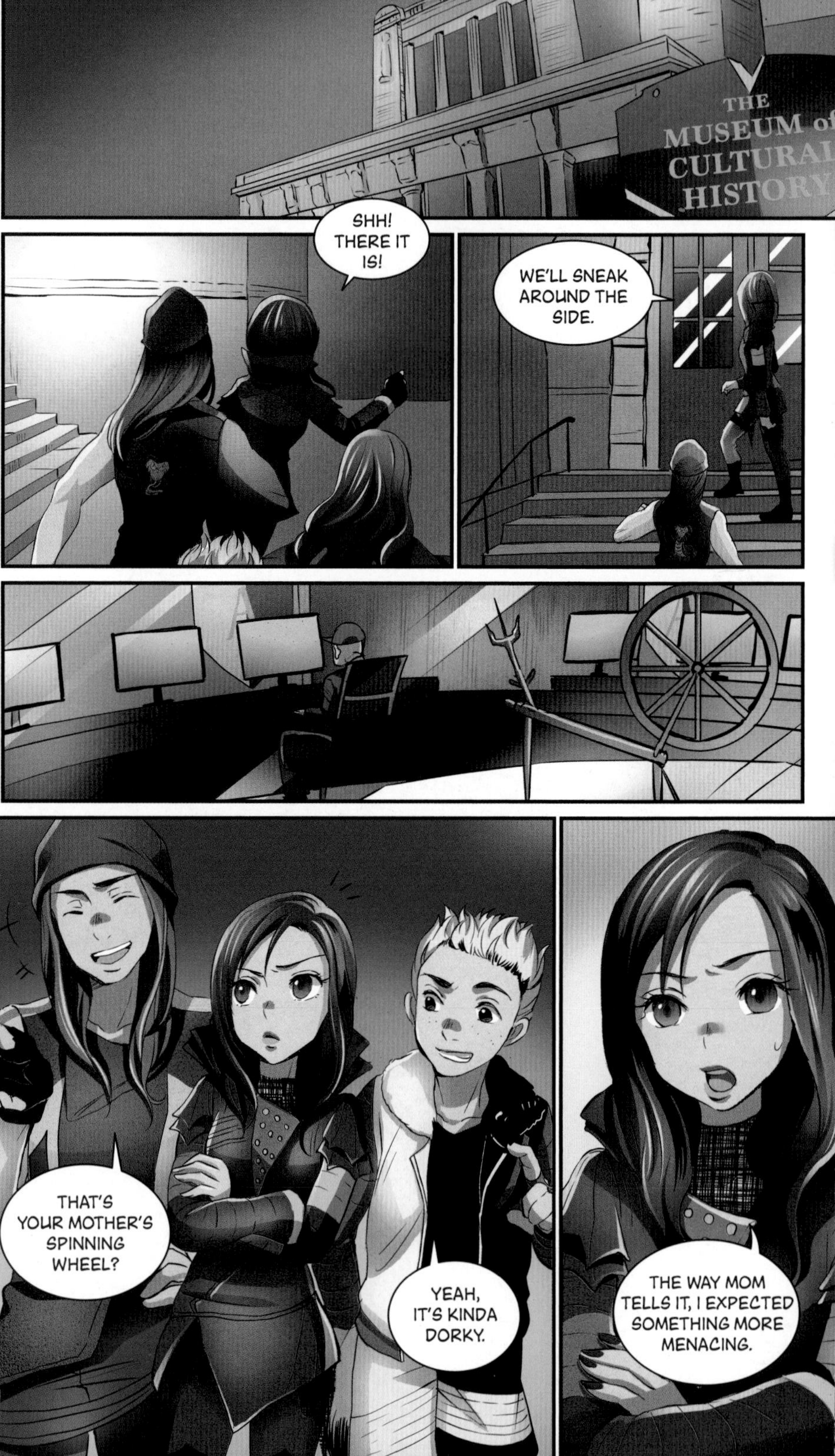
THE MUSEUM of CULTURAL HISTORY
SHH! THERE IT IS!
WE'LL SNEAK AROUND THE SIDE.
THAT'S YOUR MOTHER'S SPINNING WHEEL?
YEAH, IT'S KINDA DORKY.
THE WAY MOM TELLS IT, I EXPECTED SOMETHING MORE MENACING.

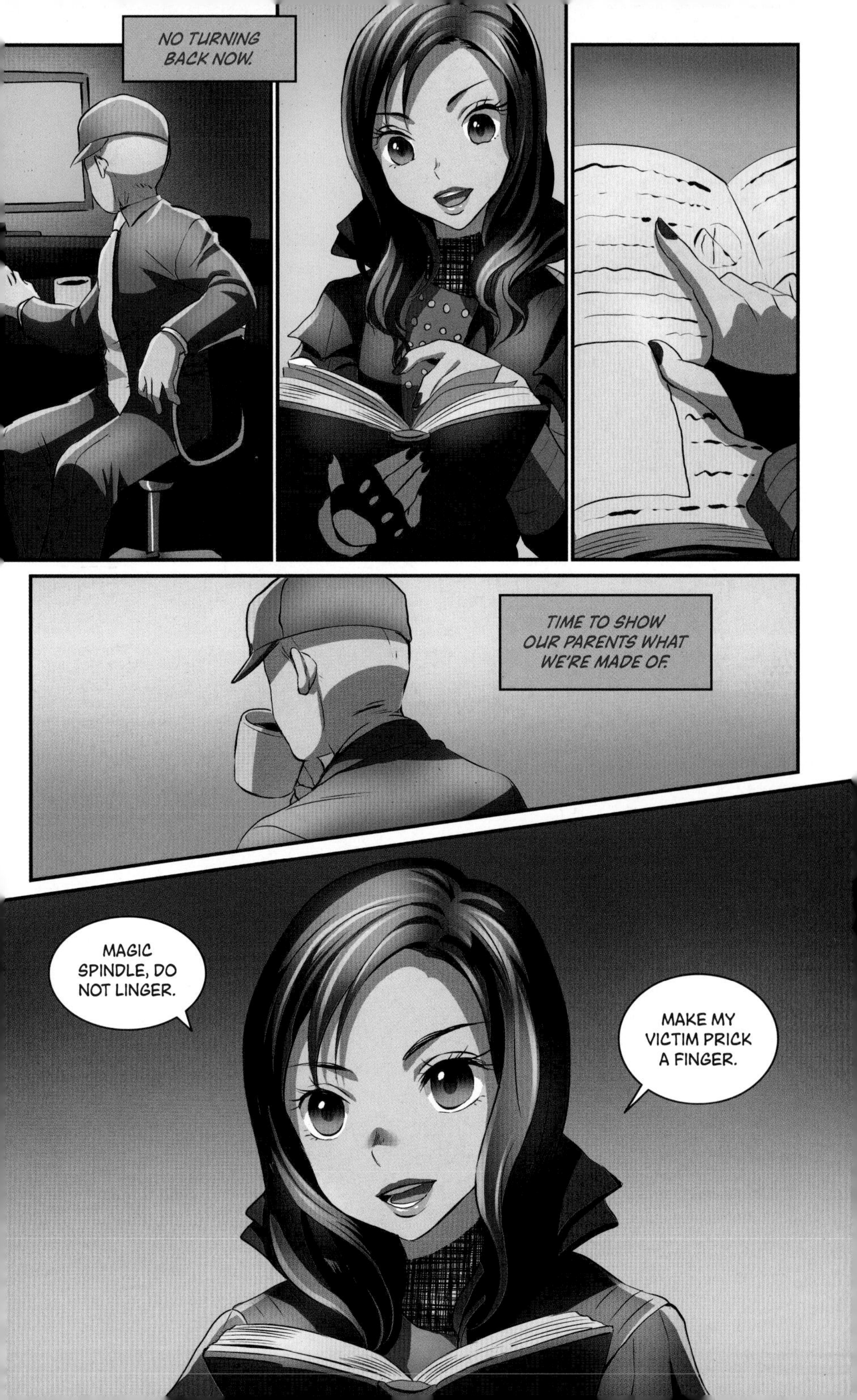
NO TURNING BACK NOW.
TIME TO SHOW OUR PARENTS WHAT WE'RE MADE OF.
MAGIC SPINDLE, DO NOT LINGER.
MAKE MY VICTIM PRICK A FINGER.

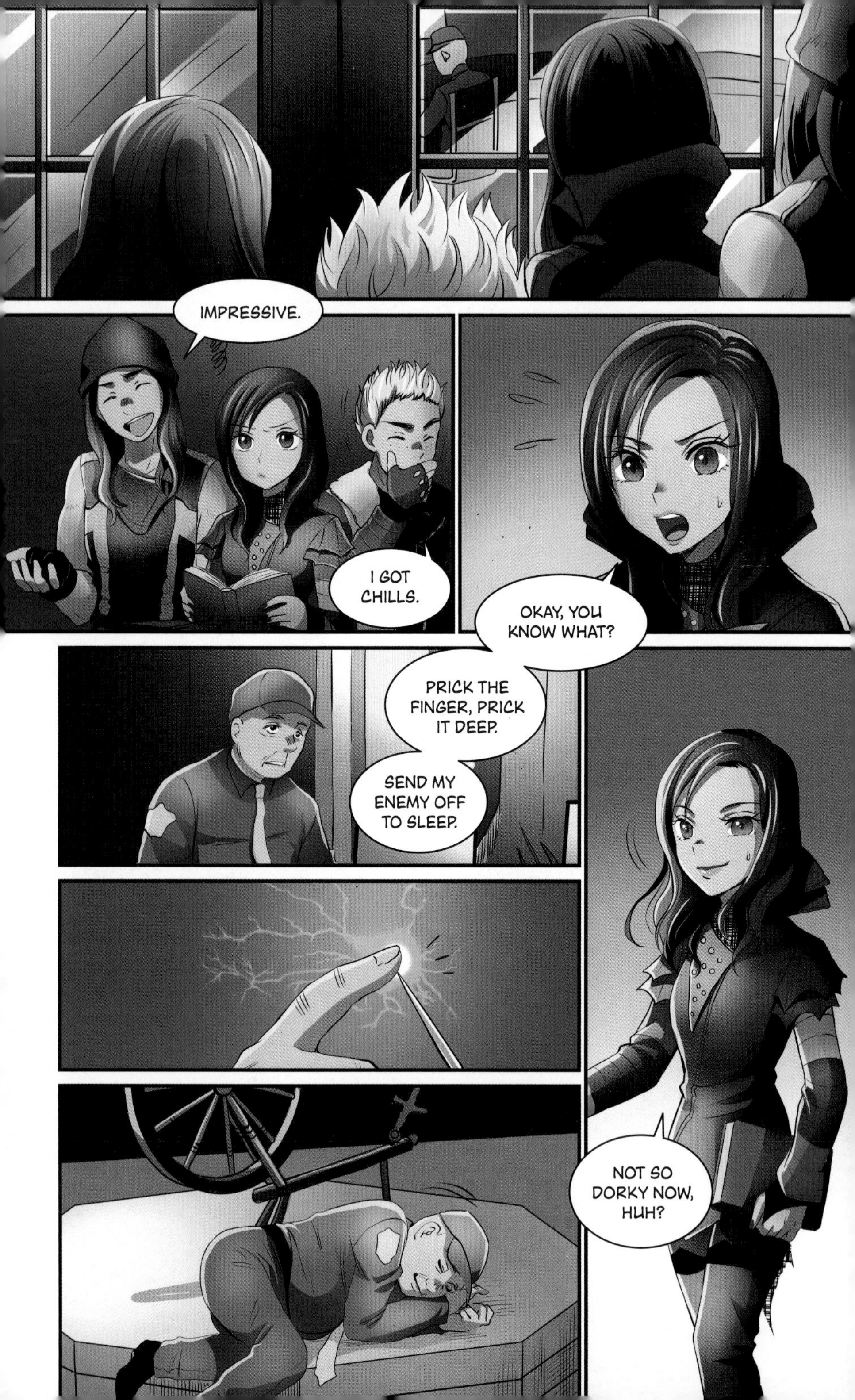
IMPRESSIVE.
I GOT CHILLS.
OKAY, YOU KNOW WHAT?
PRICK THE FINGER, PRICK IT DEEP.
SEND MY ENEMY OFF TO SLEEP.
NOT SO DORKY NOW, HUH?

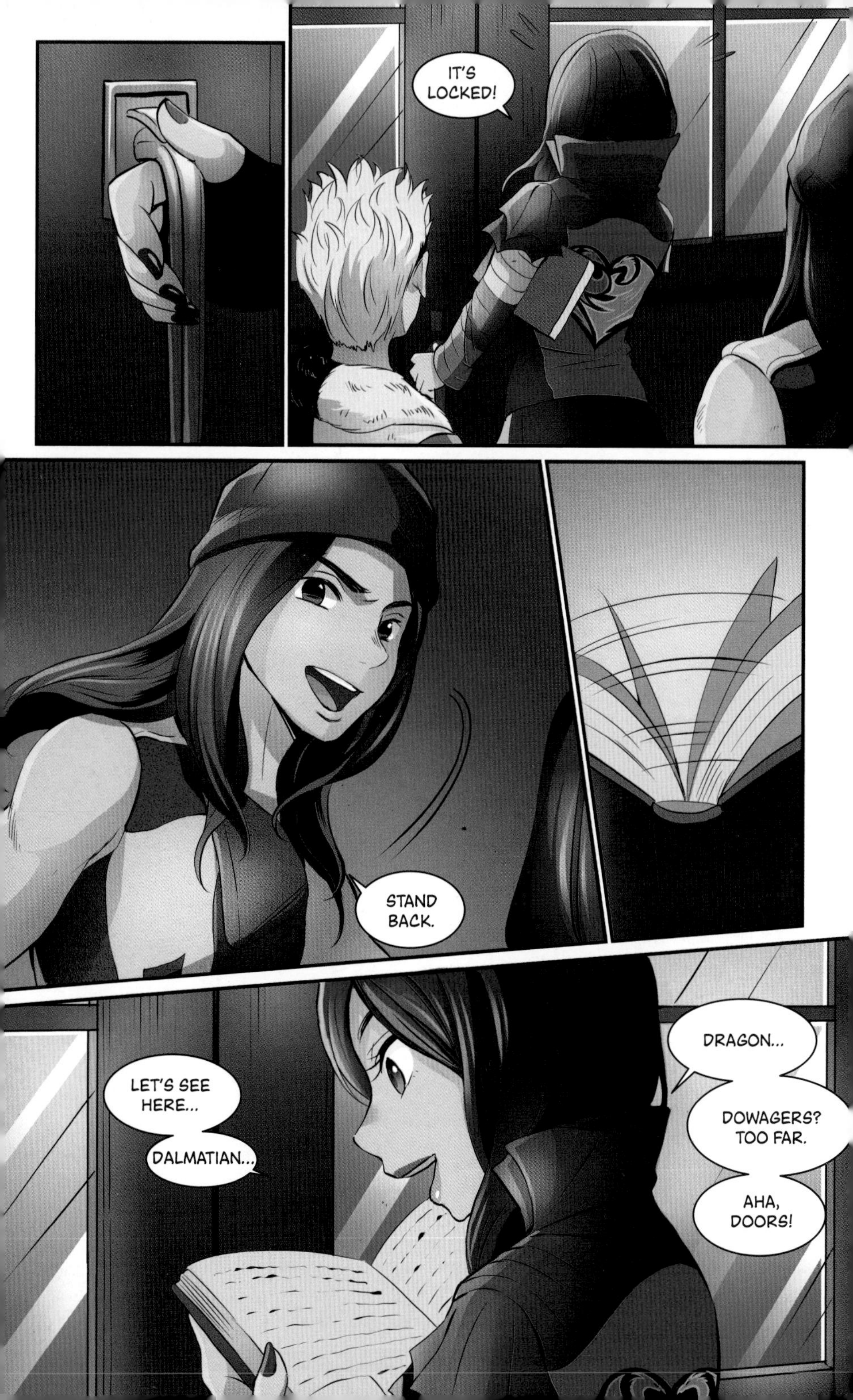
IT'S LOCKED!
STAND BACK.
LET'S SEE HERE...
DALMATIAN...
DRAGON...
DOWAGERS? TOO FAR.
AHA, DOORS!

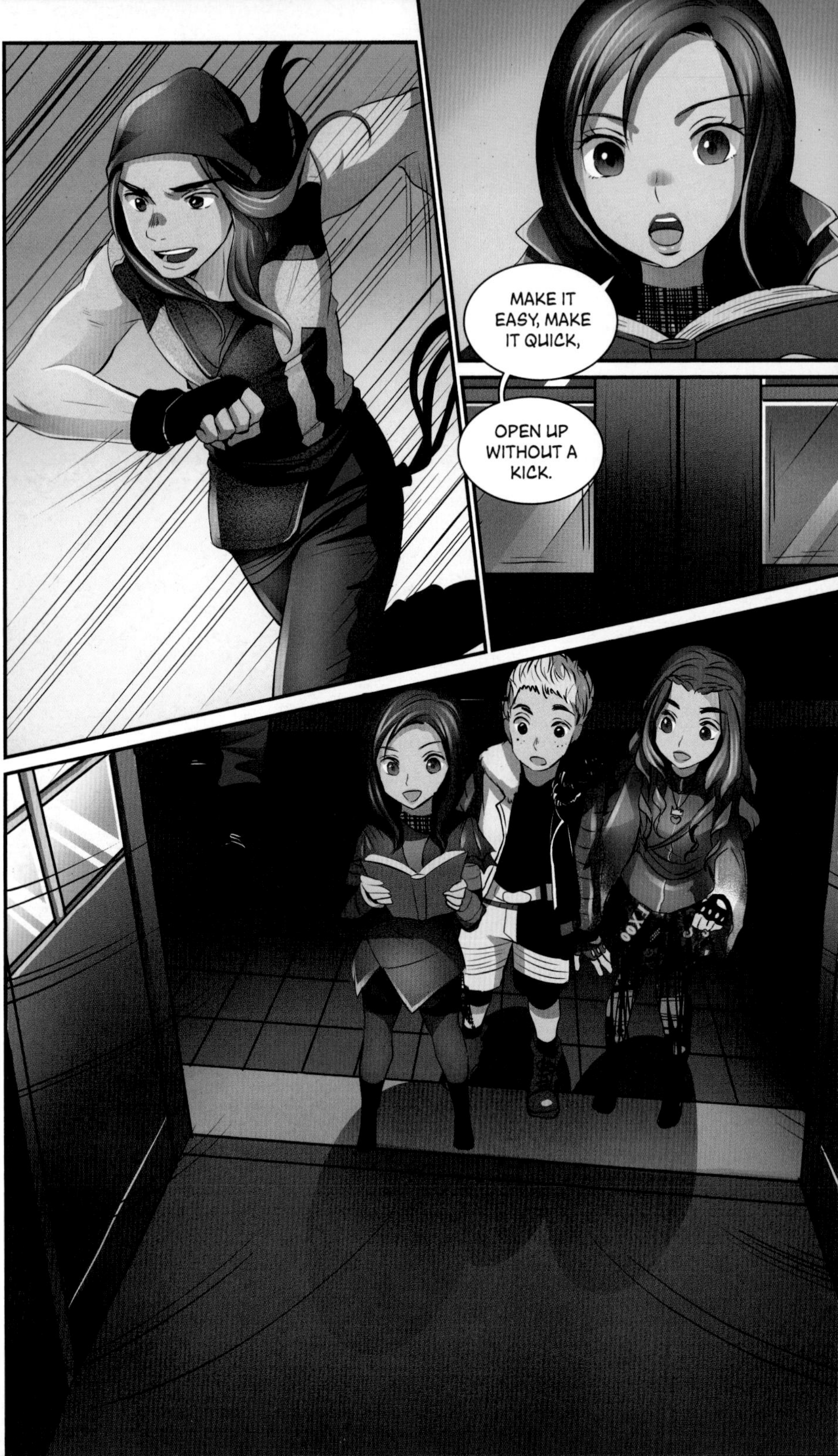
MAKE IT EASY, MAKE IT QUICK,
OPEN UP WITHOUT A KICK.

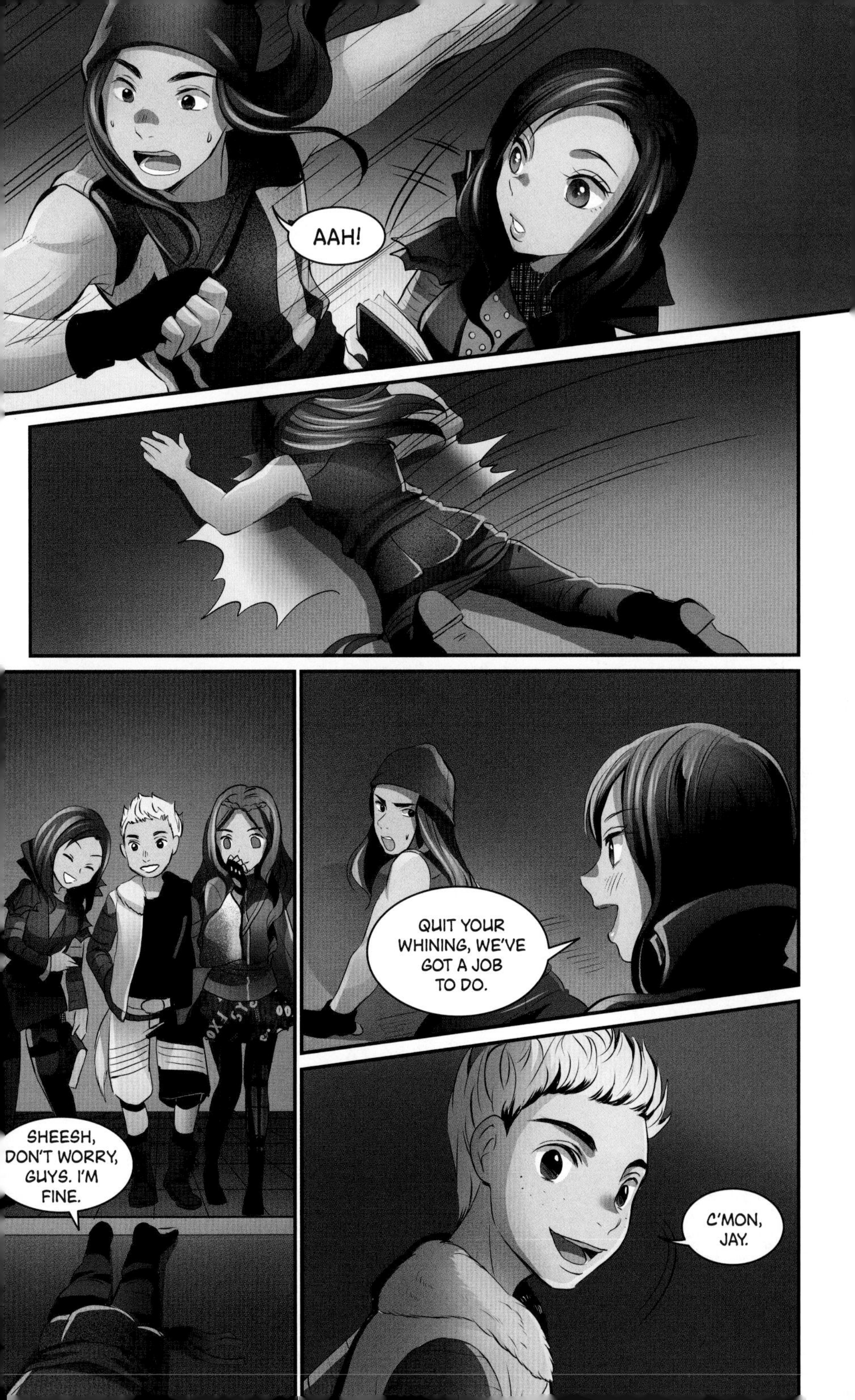
AAH!
SHEESH, DON'T WORRY, GUYS. I'M FINE.
QUIT YOUR WHINING, WE'VE GOT A JOB TO DO.
C'MON, JAY.

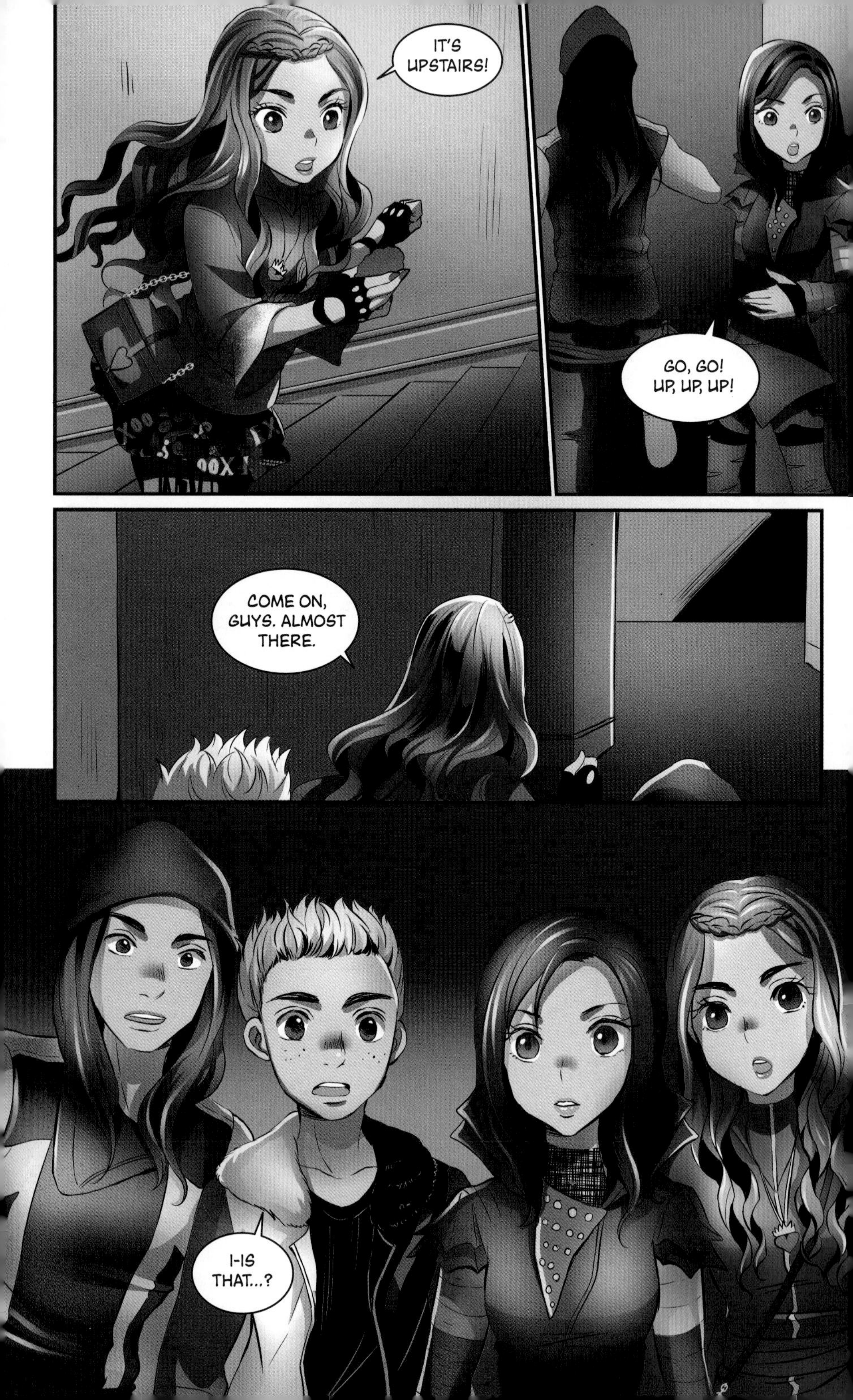
IT'S UPSTAIRS!
GO, GO! UP, UP, UP!
COME ON, GUYS. ALMOST THERE.
I-IS THAT...?

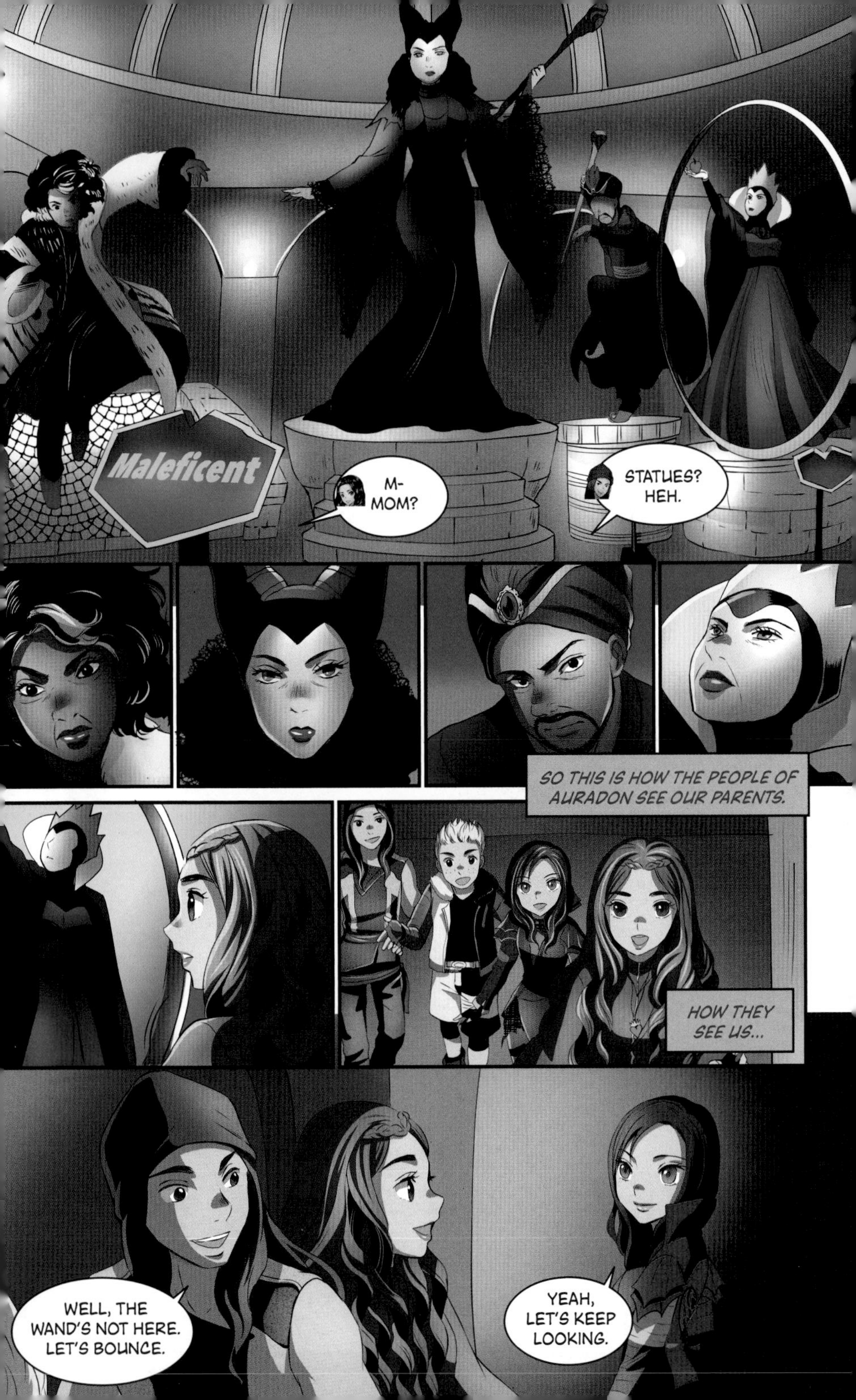
Maleficent
M-
MOM?
STATUES?
HEH.
SO THIS IS HOW THE PEOPLE OF AURADON SEE OUR PARENTS.
HOW THEY SEE US...
WELL, THE WAND'S NOT HERE. LET'S BOUNCE.
YEAH, LET'S KEEP LOOKING.

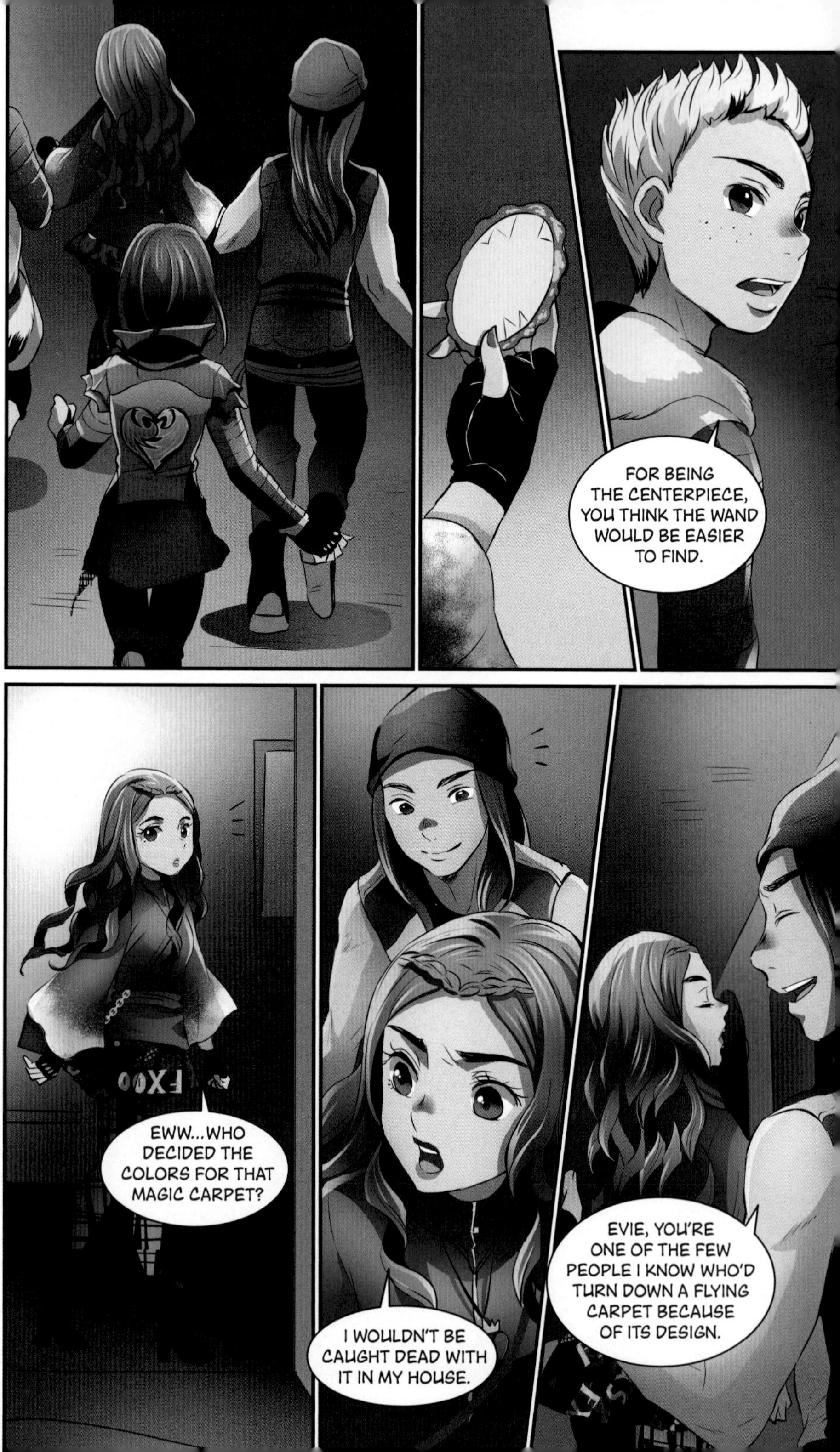
FOR BEING THE CENTERPIECE, YOU THINK THE WAND WOULD BE EASIER TO FIND.
EWW...WHO DECIDED THE COLORS FOR THAT MAGIC CARPET?
I WOULDN'T BE CAUGHT DEAD WITH IT IN MY HOUSE.
EVIE, YOU'RE ONE OF THE FEW PEOPLE I KNOW WHO'D TURN DOWN A FLYING CARPET BECAUSE OF ITS DESIGN.

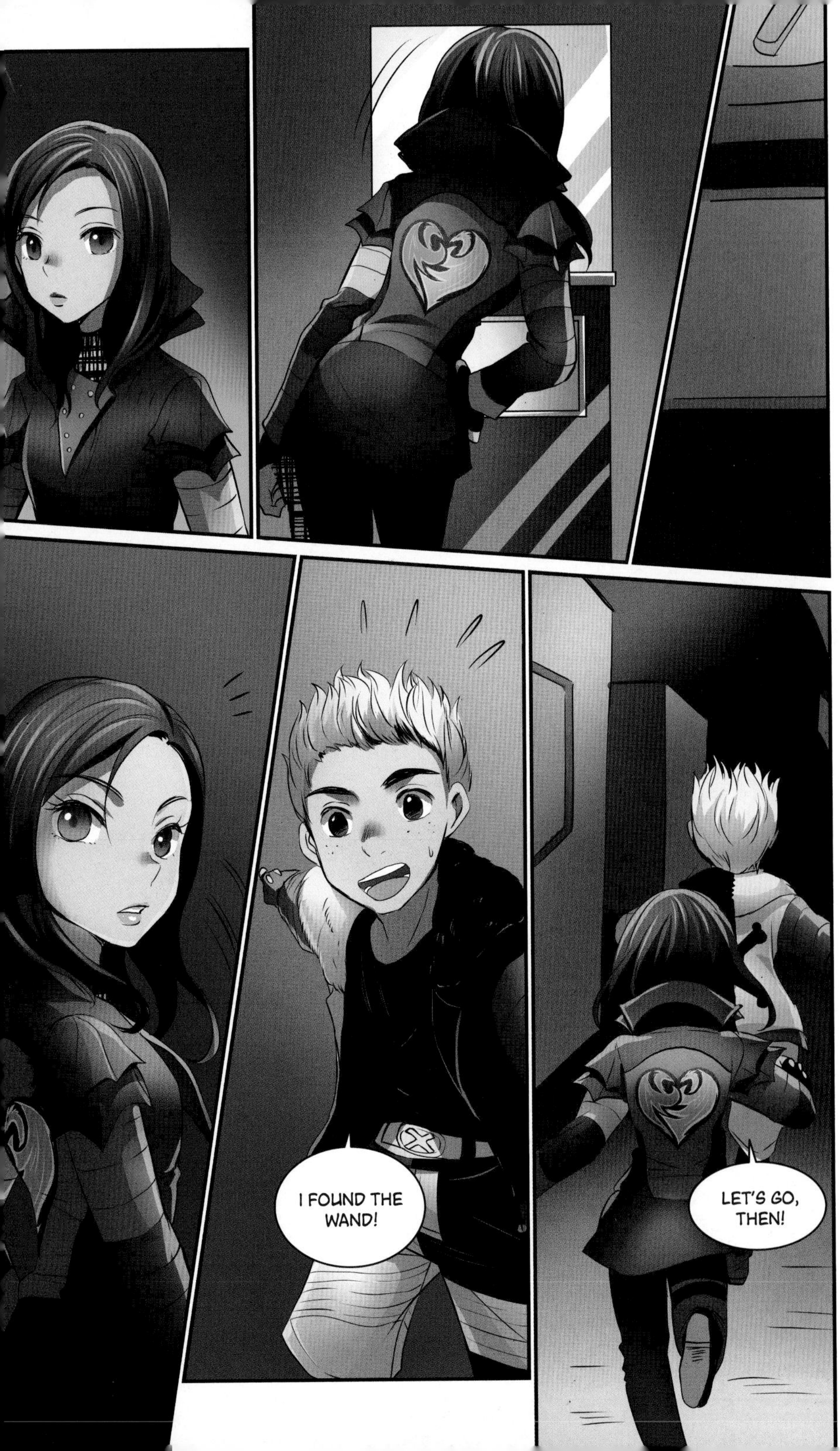
I FOUND THE WAND!
LET'S GO, THEN!

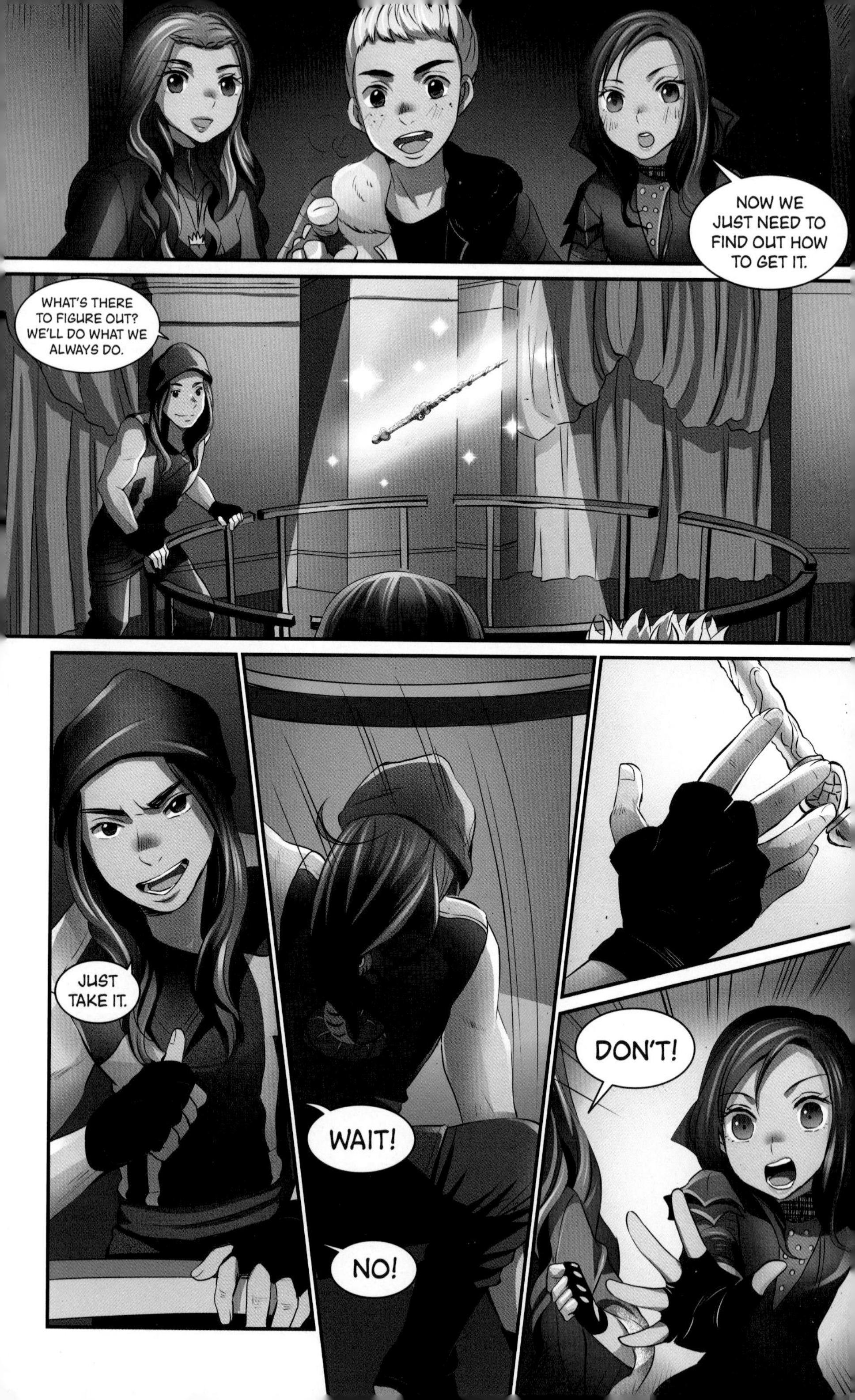
NOW WE JUST NEED TO FIND OUT HOW TO GET IT.
WHAT'S THERE TO FIGURE OUT? WE'LL DO WHAT WE ALWAYS DO.
JUST TAKE IT.
WAIT!
NO!
DON'T!

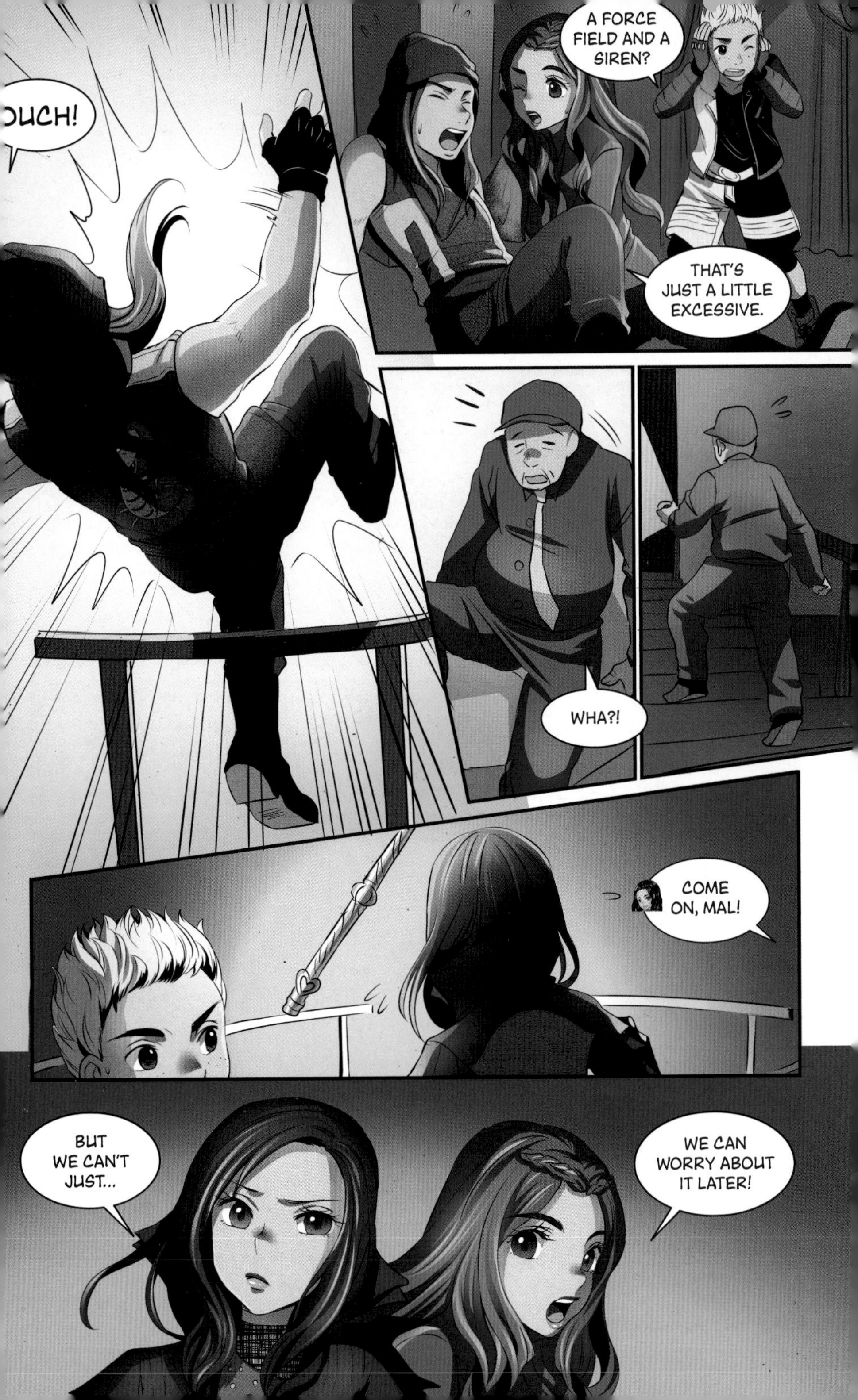
OUCH!
A FORCE FIELD AND A SIREN?
THAT'S JUST A LITTLE EXCESSIVE.
WHA?!
COME ON, MAL!
BUT WE CAN'T JUST...
WE CAN WORRY ABOUT IT LATER!

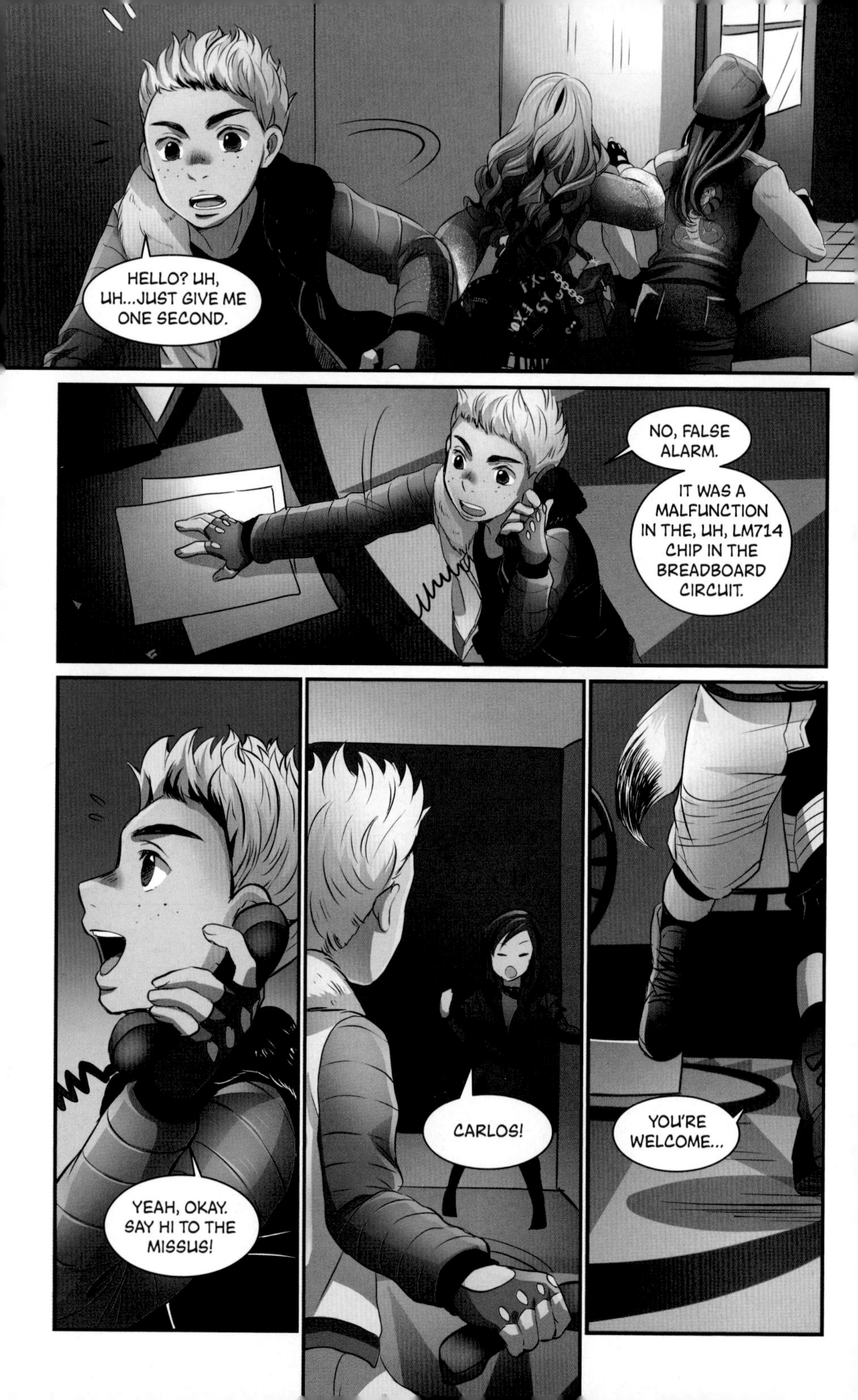
HELLO? UH, UH...JUST GIVE ME ONE SECOND.
NO, FALSE ALARM.
IT WAS A MALFUNCTION IN THE, UH, LM714 CHIP IN THE BREADBOARD CIRCUIT.
YEAH, OKAY. SAY HI TO THE MISSUS!
CARLOS!
YOU'RE WELCOME...

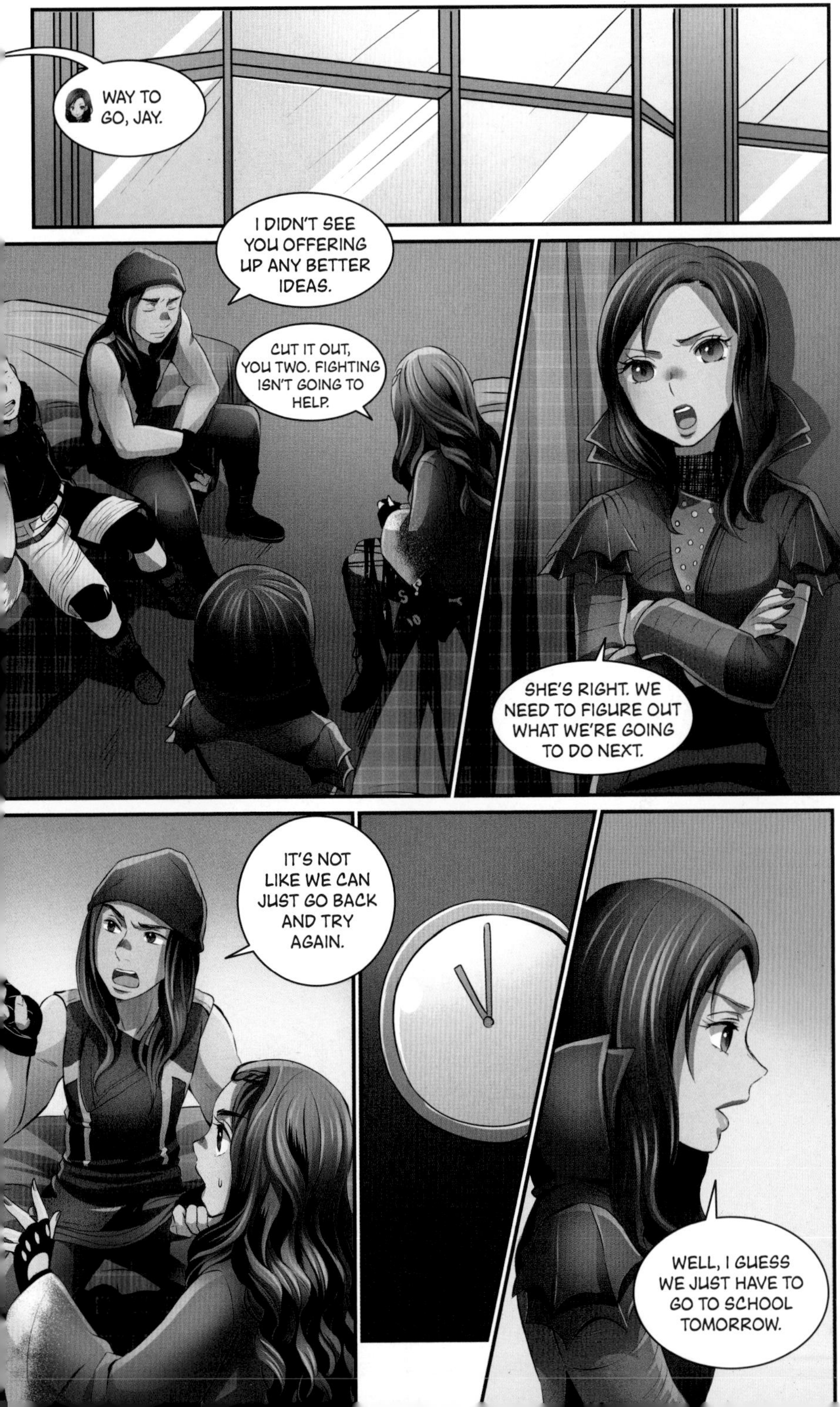
WAY TO GO, JAY.
I DIDN'T SEE YOU OFFERING UP ANY BETTER IDEAS.
CUT IT OUT, YOU TWO. FIGHTING ISN'T GOING TO HELP.
SHE'S RIGHT. WE NEED TO FIGURE OUT WHAT WE'RE GOING TO DO NEXT.
IT'S NOT LIKE WE CAN JUST GO BACK AND TRY AGAIN.
WELL, I GUESS WE JUST HAVE TO GO TO SCHOOL TOMORROW.

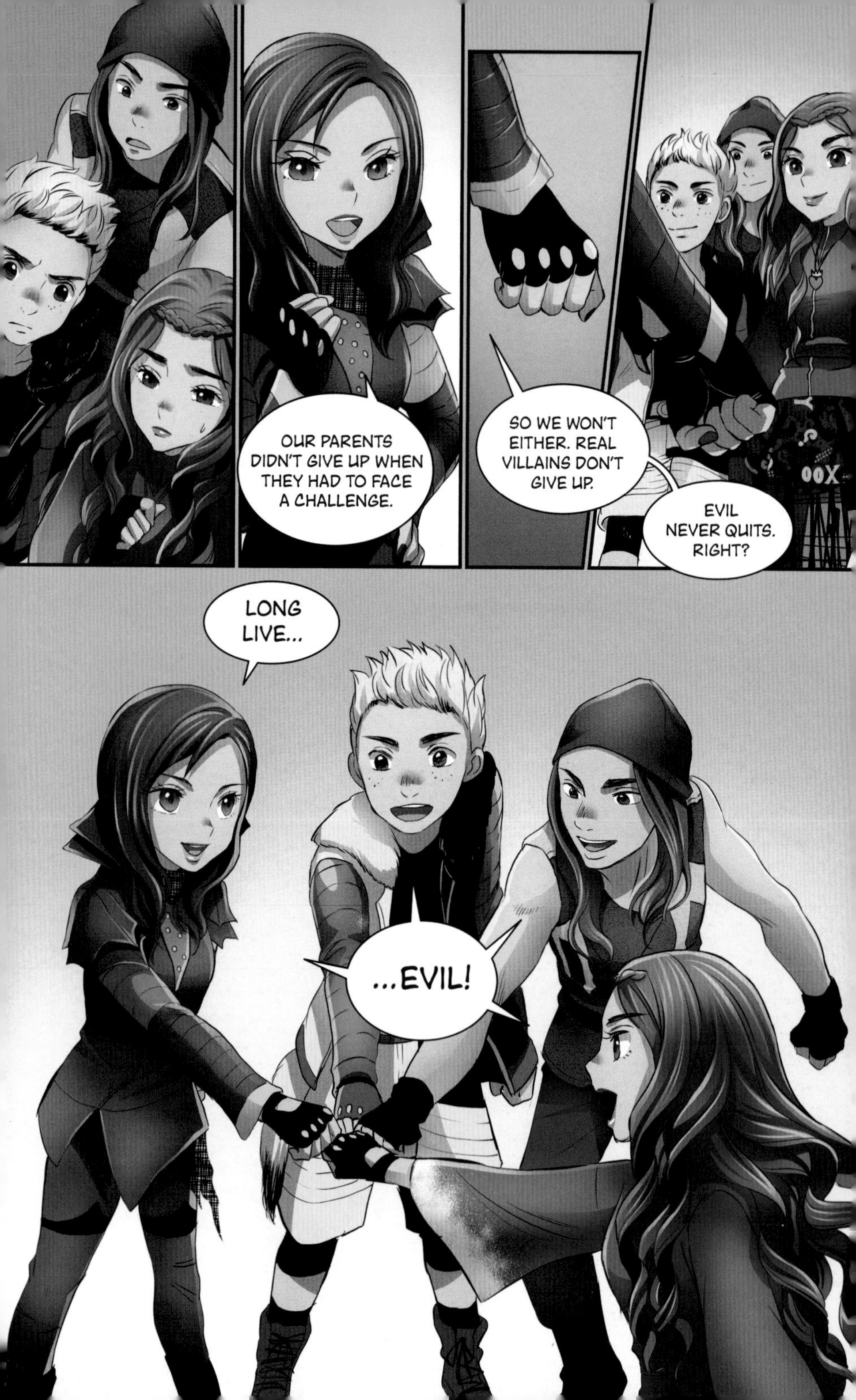
OUR PARENTS DIDN'T GIVE UP WHEN THEY HAD TO FACE A CHALLENGE.
SO WE WON'T EITHER. REAL VILLAINS DON'T GIVE UP.
EVIL NEVER QUITS. RIGHT?
LONG LIVE...
...EVIL!

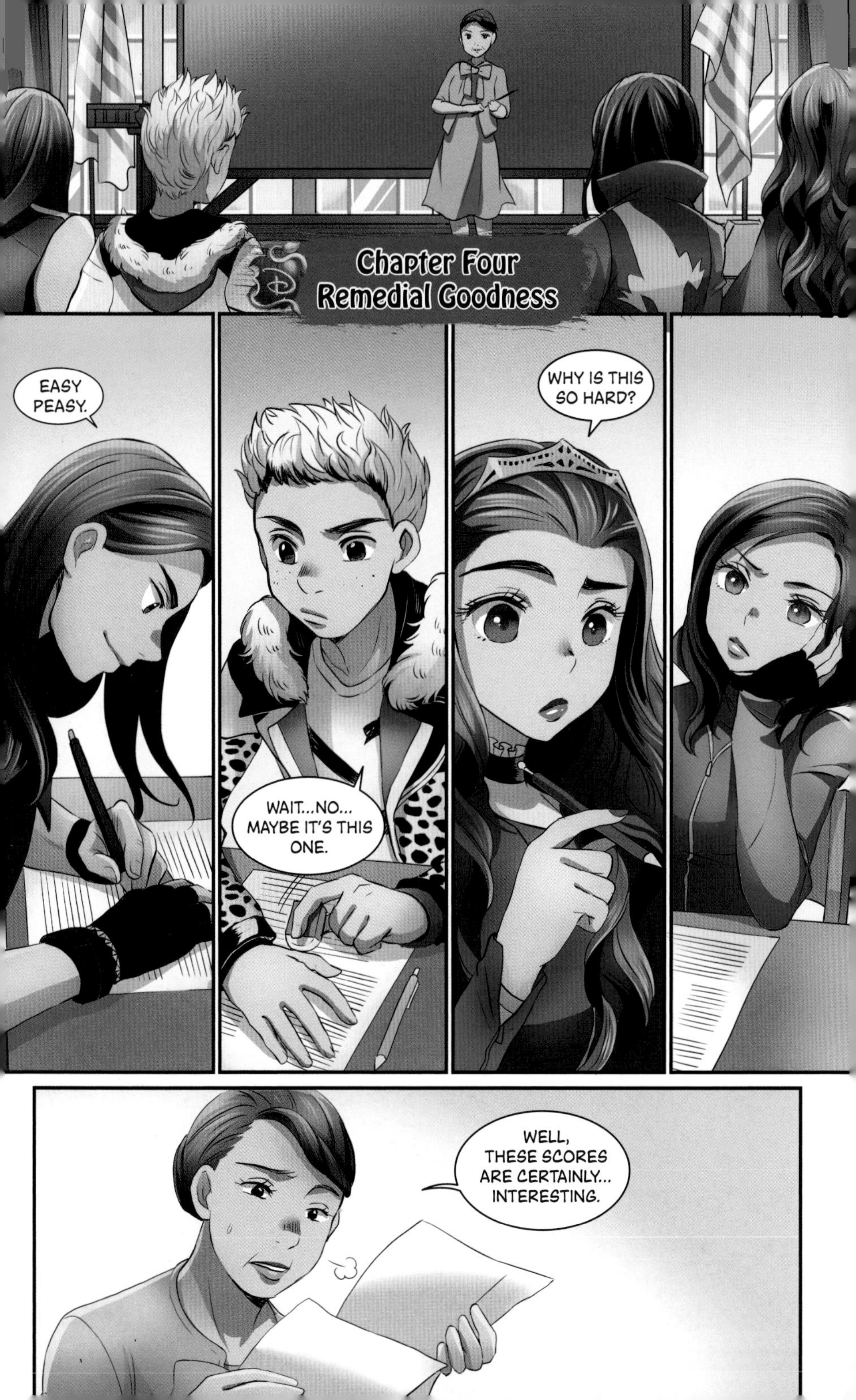
Chapter Four
Remedial Goodness
EASY PEASY.
WAIT...NO... MAYBE IT'S THIS ONE.
WHY IS THIS SO HARD?
WELL, THESE SCORES ARE CERTAINLY... INTERESTING.

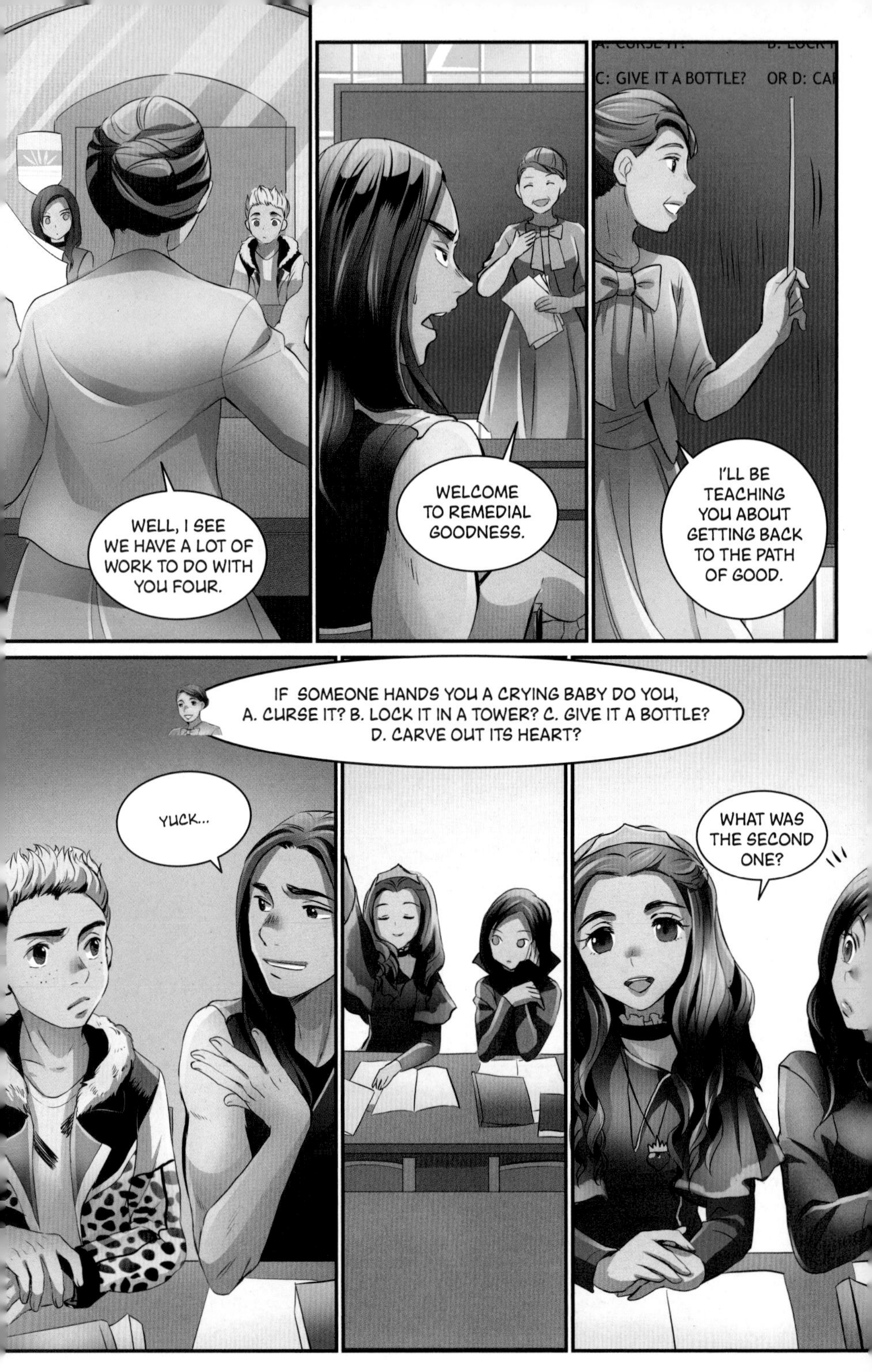
WELL, I SEE WE HAVE A LOT OF WORK TO DO WITH YOU FOUR.
WELCOME TO REMEDIAL GOODNESS.
C: GIVE IT A BOTTLE? OR D:
I'LL BE TEACHING YOU ABOUT GETTING BACK TO THE PATH OF GOOD.
IF SOMEONE HANDS YOU A CRYING BABY DO YOU, A. CURSE IT? B. LOCK IT IN A TOWER? C. GIVE IT A BOTTLE? D. CARVE OUT ITS HEART?
YUCK...
WHAT WAS THE SECOND ONE?

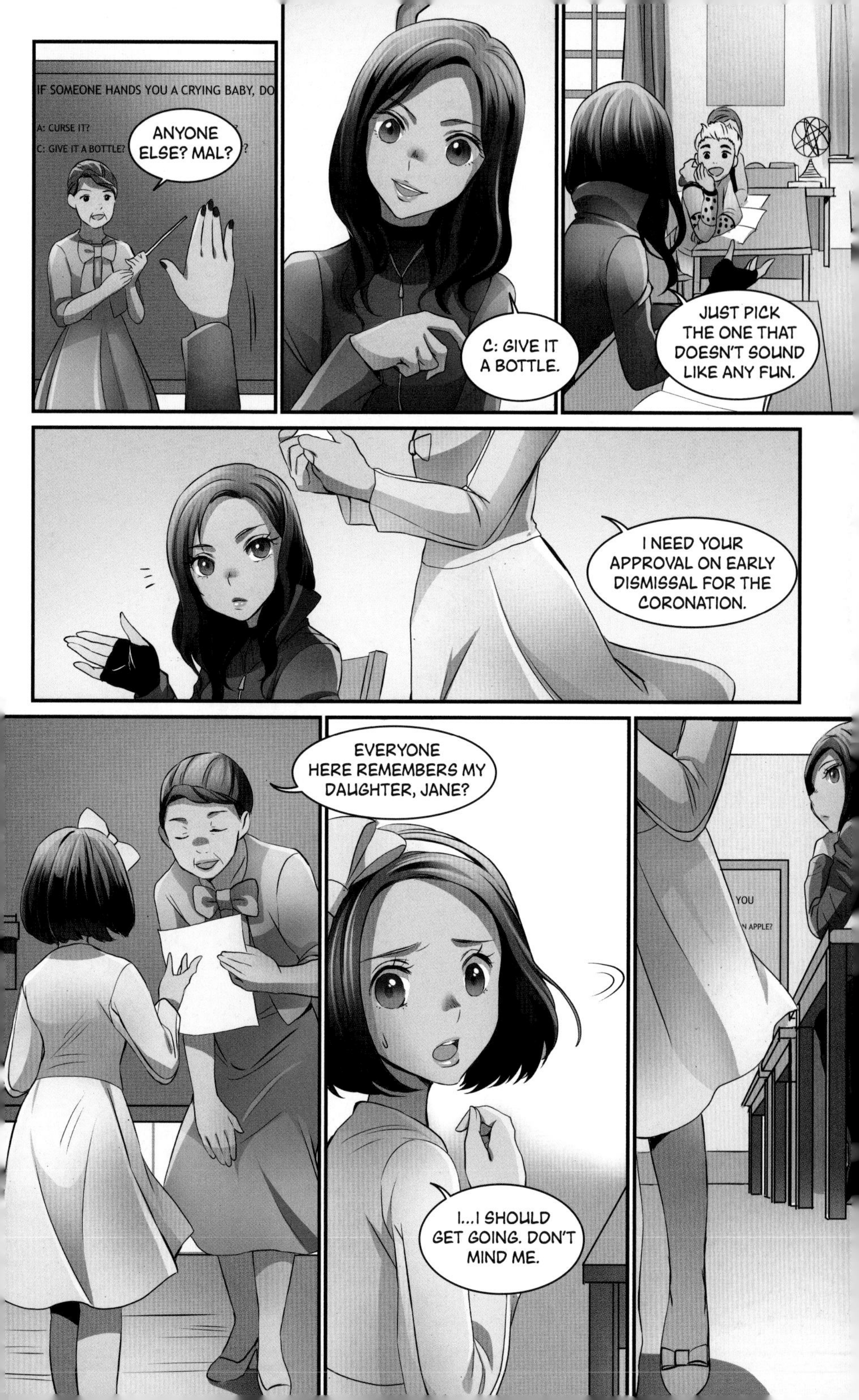
IF SOMEONE HANDS YOU A CRYING BABY, DO
A: CURSE IT?
C: GIVE IT A BOTTLE?
ANYONE ELSE? MAL?
C: GIVE IT A BOTTLE.
JUST PICK THE ONE THAT DOESN'T SOUND LIKE ANY FUN.
I NEED YOUR APPROVAL ON EARLY DISMISSAL FOR THE CORONATION.
EVERYONE HERE REMEMBERS MY DAUGHTER, JANE?
I...I SHOULD GET GOING. DON'T MIND ME.

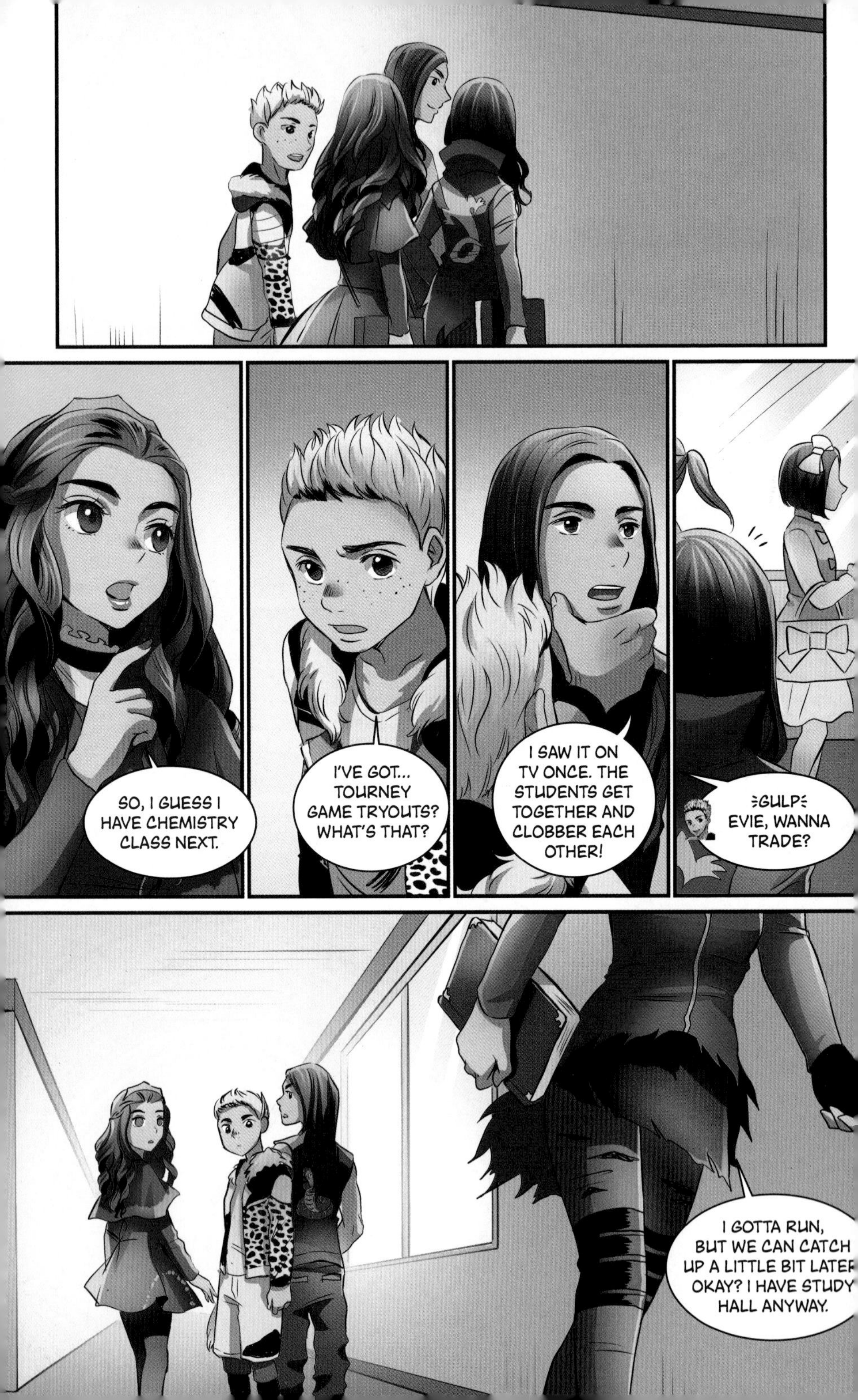
SO, I GUESS I HAVE CHEMISTRY CLASS NEXT.
I'VE GOT... TOURNEY GAME TRYOUTS? WHAT'S THAT?
I SAW IT ON TV ONCE. THE STUDENTS GET TOGETHER AND CLOBBER EACH OTHER!
GULP
EVIE, WANNA TRADE?
I GOTTA RUN, BUT WE CAN CATCH UP A LITTLE BIT LATER OKAY? I HAVE STUDY HALL ANYWAY.

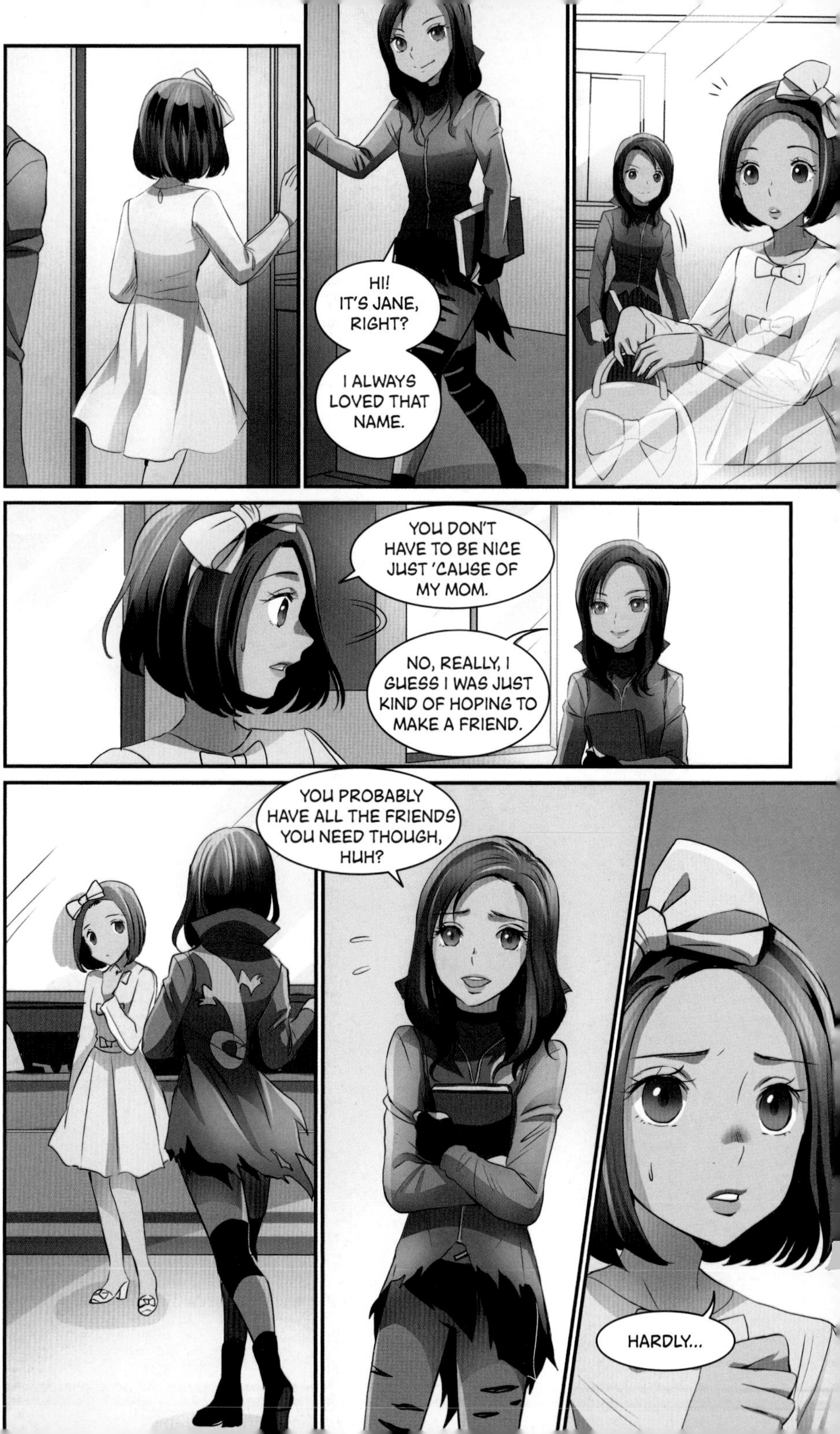
HI! IT'S JANE, RIGHT?
I ALWAYS LOVED THAT NAME.
YOU DON'T HAVE TO BE NICE JUST 'CAUSE OF MY MOM.
NO, REALLY, I GUESS I WAS JUST KIND OF HOPING TO MAKE A FRIEND.
YOU PROBABLY HAVE ALL THE FRIENDS YOU NEED THOUGH, HUH?
HARDLY...

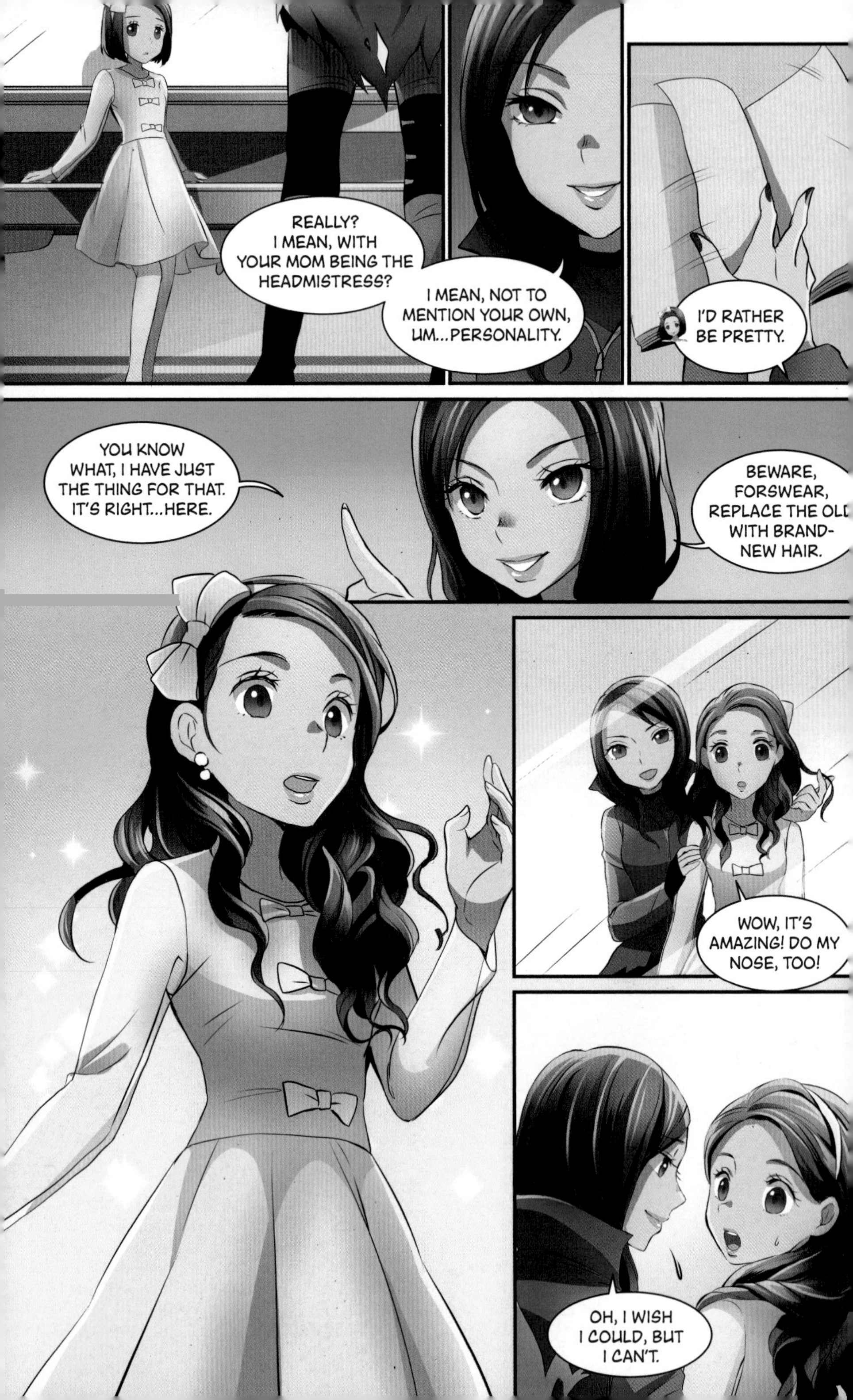
REALLY? I MEAN, WITH YOUR MOM BEING THE HEADMISTRESS?
I MEAN, NOT TO MENTION YOUR OWN, UM...PERSONALITY.
I'D RATHER BE PRETTY.
YOU KNOW WHAT, I HAVE JUST THE THING FOR THAT. IT'S RIGHT...HERE.
BEWARE, FORSWEAR, REPLACE THE OLD WITH BRAND-NEW HAIR.
WOW, IT'S AMAZING! DO MY NOSE, TOO!
OH, I WISH I COULD, BUT I CAN'T.

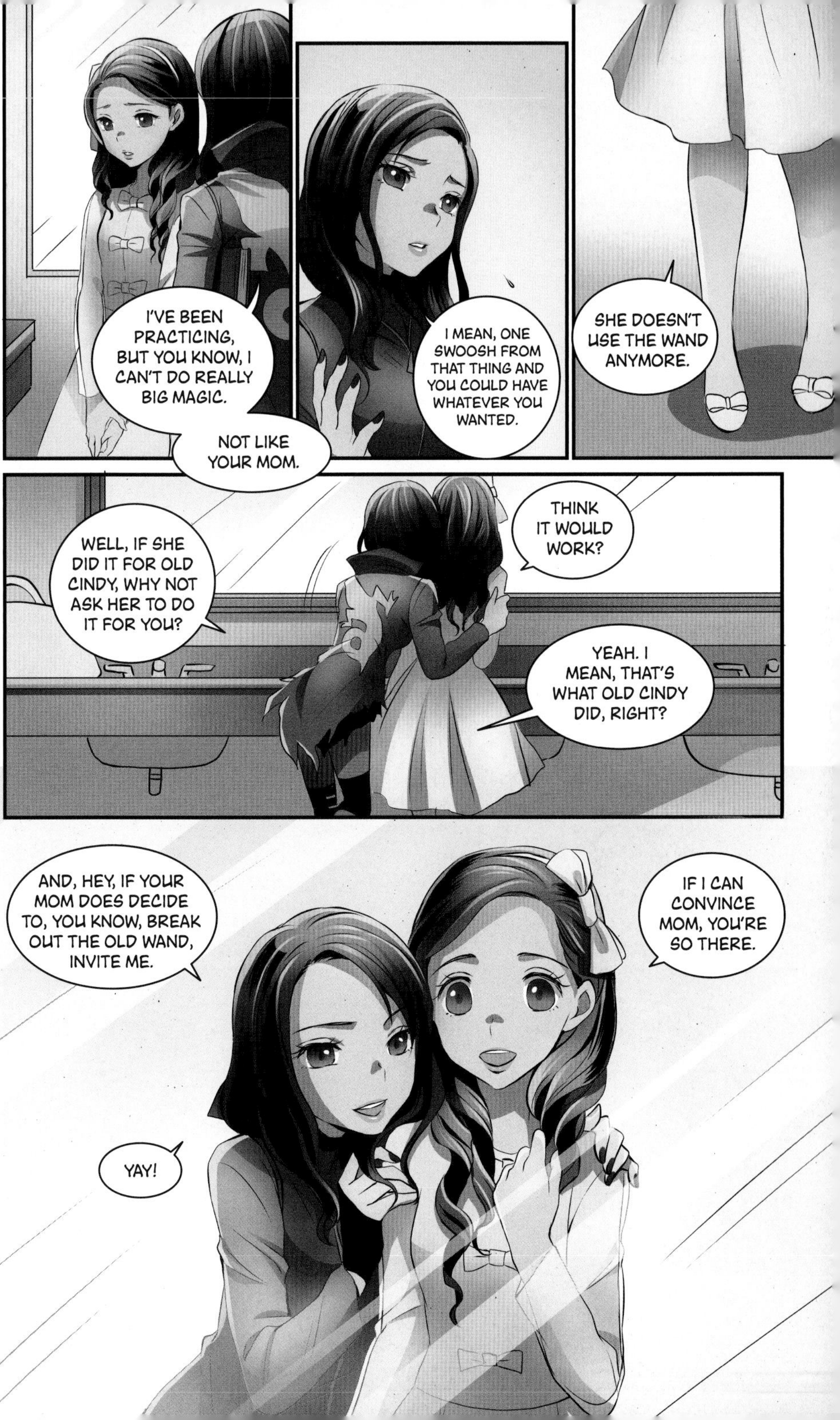
I'VE BEEN PRACTICING, BUT YOU KNOW, I CAN'T DO REALLY BIG MAGIC.
NOT LIKE YOUR MOM.
I MEAN, ONE SWOOSH FROM THAT THING AND YOU COULD HAVE WHATEVER YOU WANTED.
SHE DOESN'T USE THE WAND ANYMORE.
WELL, IF SHE DID IT FOR OLD CINDY, WHY NOT ASK HER TO DO IT FOR YOU?
THINK IT WOULD WORK?
YEAH. I MEAN, THAT'S WHAT OLD CINDY DID, RIGHT?
AND, HEY, IF YOUR MOM DOES DECIDE TO, YOU KNOW, BREAK OUT THE OLD WAND, INVITE ME.
IF I CAN CONVINCE MOM, YOU'RE SO THERE.
YAY!

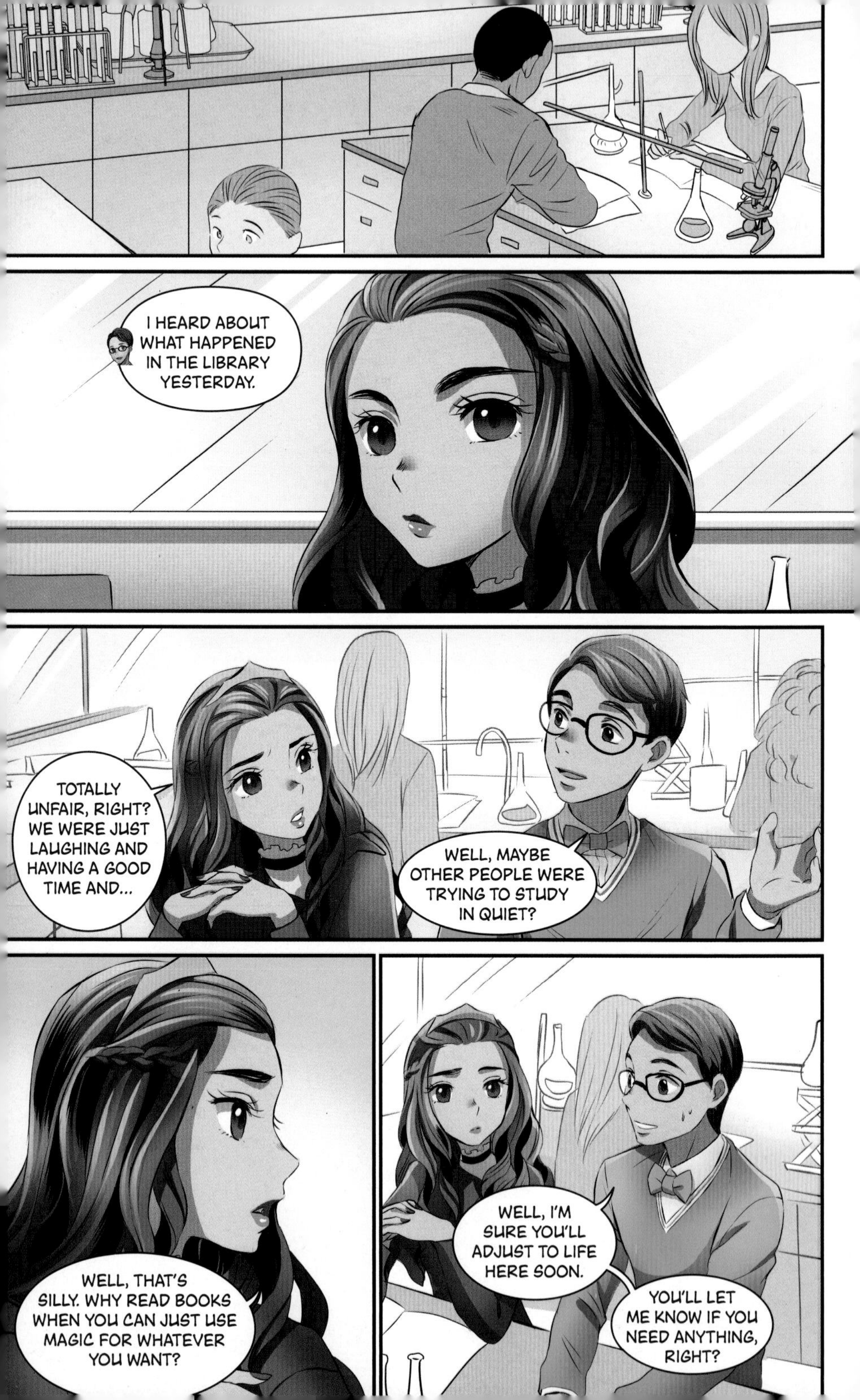
I HEARD ABOUT WHAT HAPPENED IN THE LIBRARY YESTERDAY.
TOTALLY UNFAIR, RIGHT? WE WERE JUST LAUGHING AND HAVING A GOOD TIME AND...
WELL, MAYBE OTHER PEOPLE WERE TRYING TO STUDY IN QUIET?
WELL, THAT'S SILLY. WHY READ BOOKS WHEN YOU CAN JUST USE MAGIC FOR WHATEVER YOU WANT?
WELL, I'M SURE YOU'LL ADJUST TO LIFE HERE SOON.
YOU'LL LET ME KNOW IF YOU NEED ANYTHING, RIGHT?

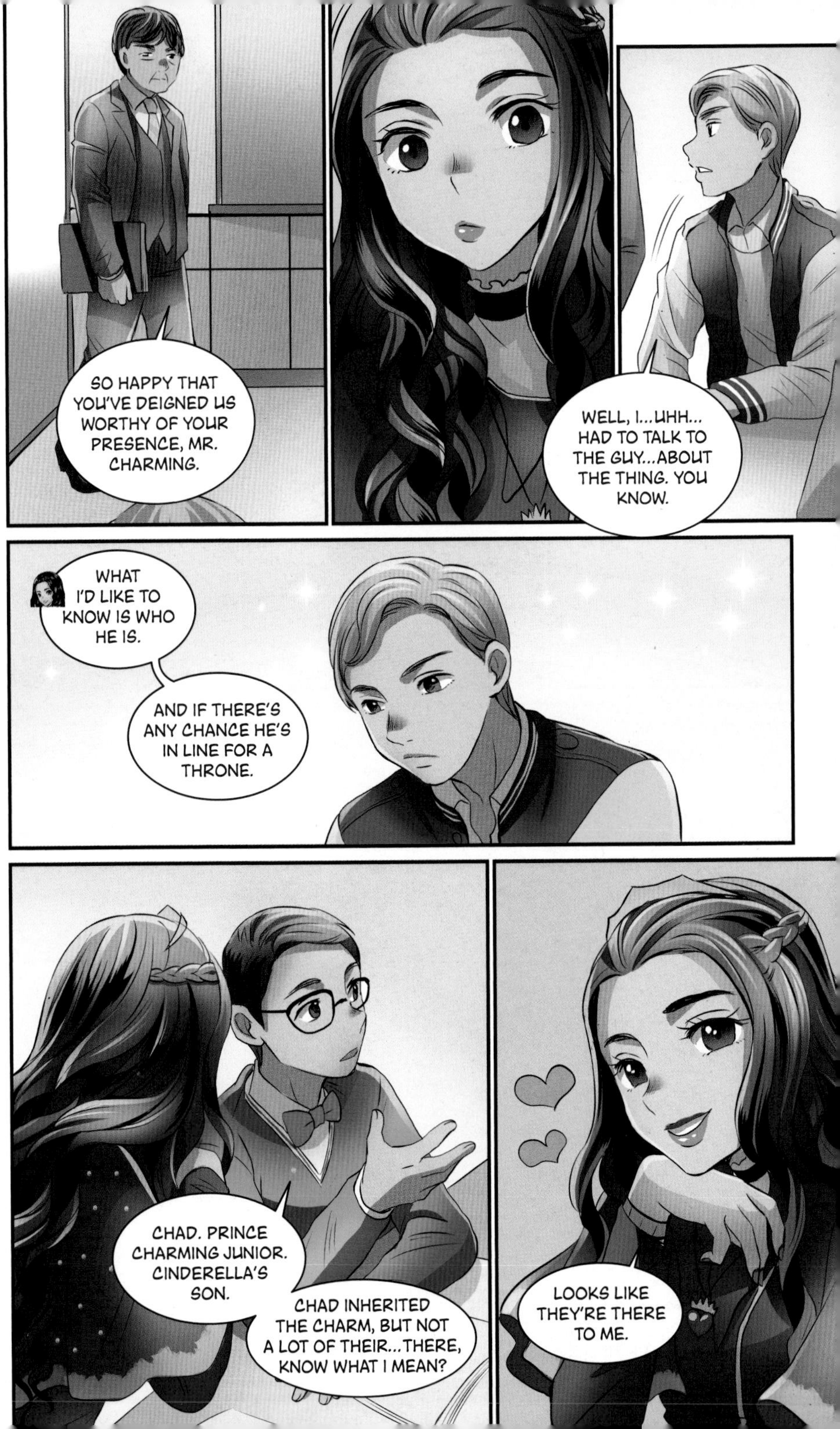
SO HAPPY THAT YOU'VE DEIGNED US WORTHY OF YOUR PRESENCE, MR. CHARMING.
WELL, I...UHH... HAD TO TALK TO THE GUY...ABOUT THE THING. YOU KNOW.
WHAT I'D LIKE TO KNOW IS WHO HE IS.
AND IF THERE'S ANY CHANCE HE'S IN LINE FOR A THRONE.
CHAD. PRINCE CHARMING JUNIOR. CINDERELLA'S SON.
CHAD INHERITED THE CHARM, BUT NOT A LOT OF THEIR...THERE, KNOW WHAT I MEAN?
LOOKS LIKE THEY'RE THERE TO ME.

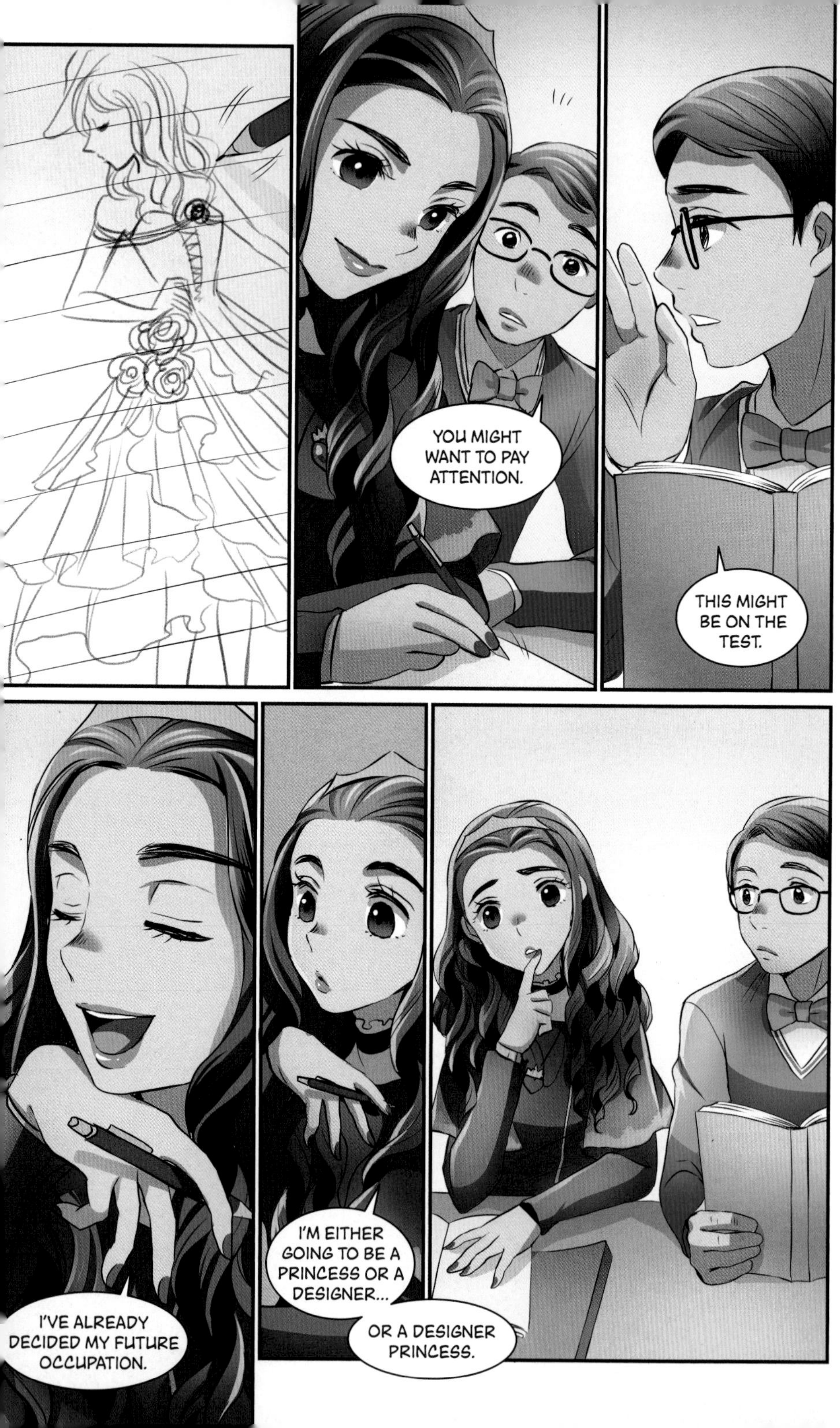
YOU MIGHT WANT TO PAY ATTENTION.
THIS MIGHT BE ON THE TEST.
I'VE ALREADY DECIDED MY FUTURE OCCUPATION.
I'M EITHER GOING TO BE A PRINCESS OR A DESIGNER...
OR A DESIGNER PRINCESS.

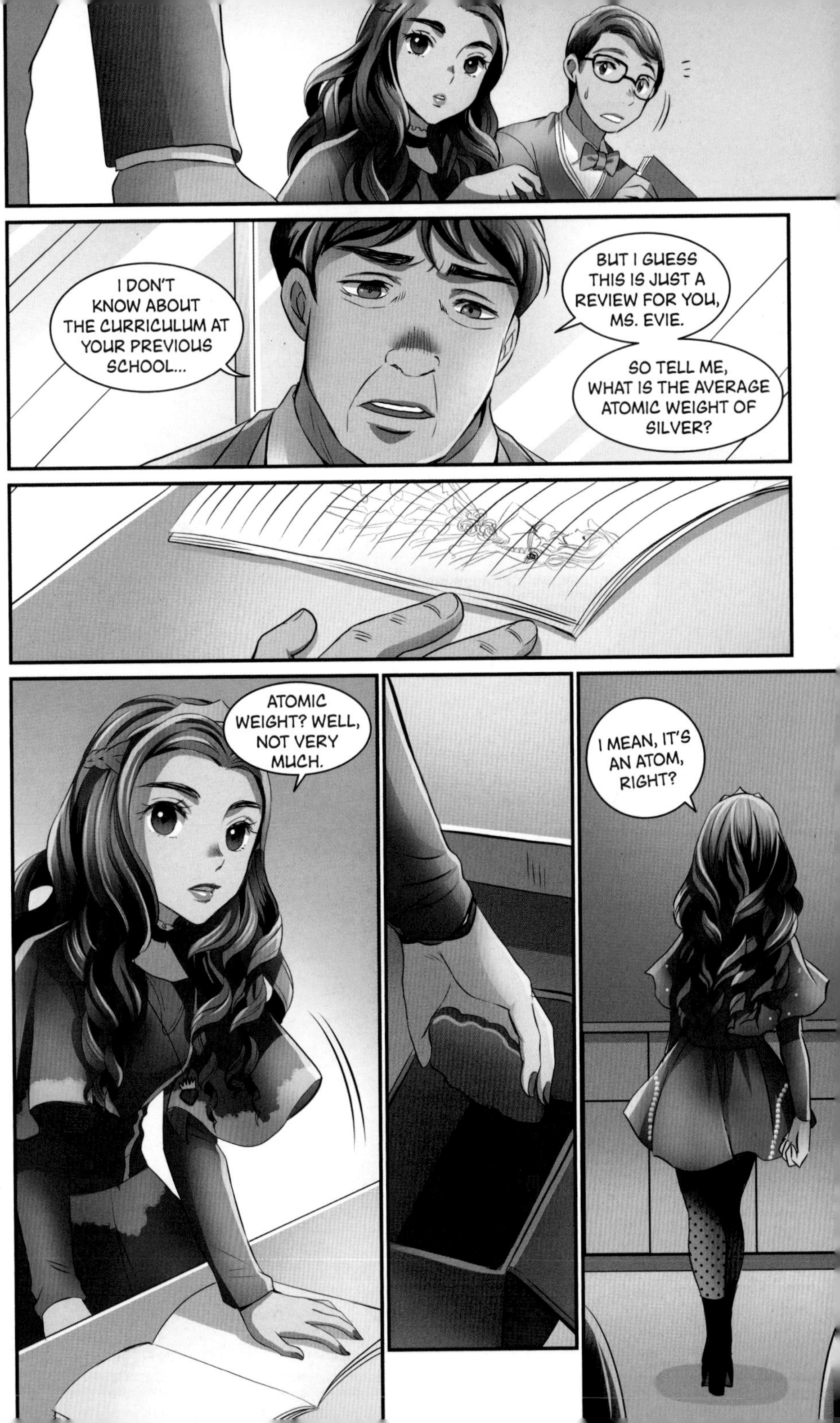
I DON'T KNOW ABOUT THE CURRICULUM AT YOUR PREVIOUS SCHOOL...
BUT I GUESS THIS IS JUST A REVIEW FOR YOU, MS. EVIE.
SO TELL ME, WHAT IS THE AVERAGE ATOMIC WEIGHT OF SILVER?
ATOMIC WEIGHT? WELL, NOT VERY MUCH.
I MEAN, IT'S AN ATOM, RIGHT?

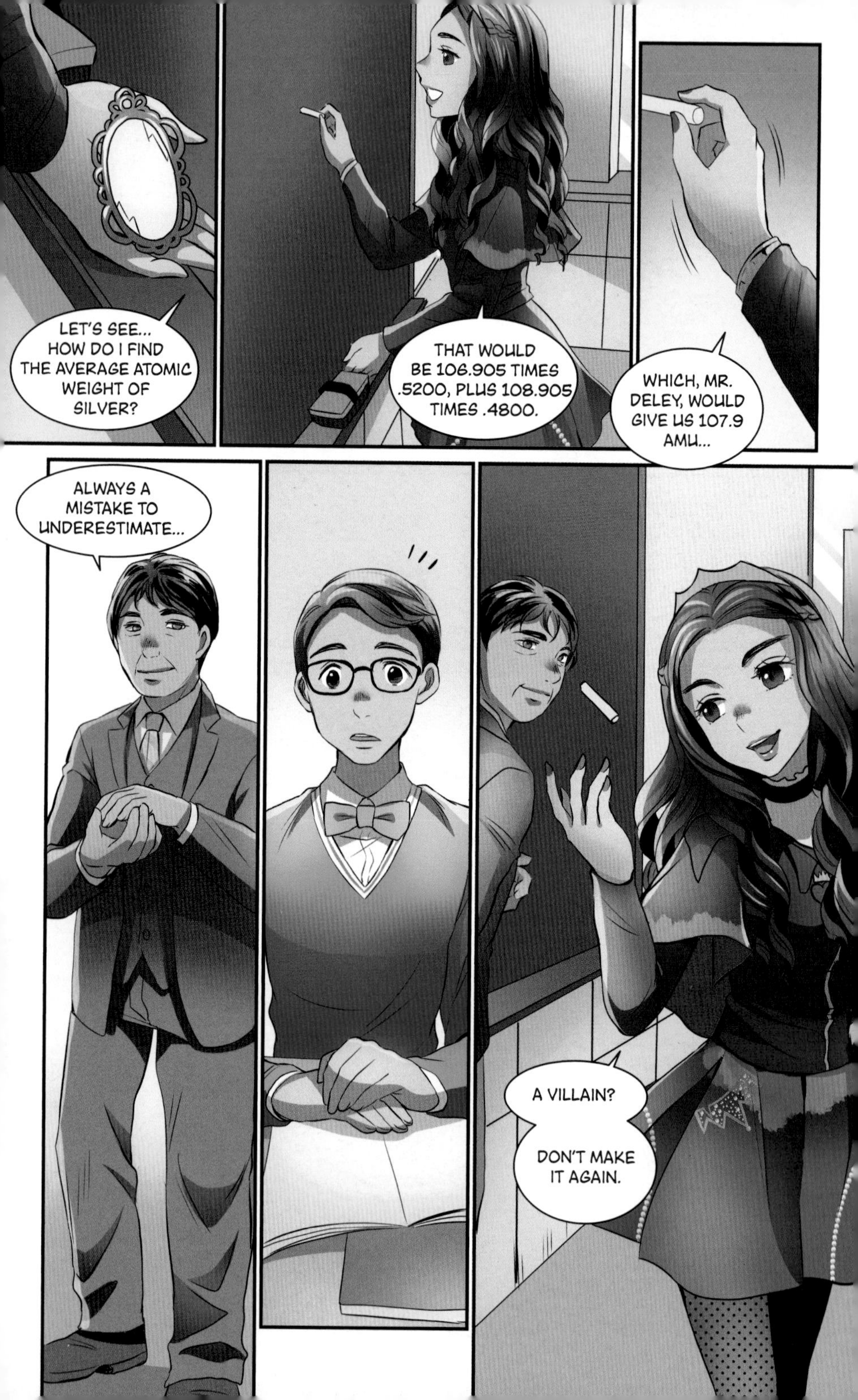
LET'S SEE... HOW DO I FIND THE AVERAGE ATOMIC WEIGHT OF SILVER?
THAT WOULD BE 106.905 TIMES .5200, PLUS 108.905 TIMES .4800.
WHICH, MR. DELEY, WOULD GIVE US 107.9 AMU...
ALWAYS A MISTAKE TO UNDERESTIMATE...
A VILLAIN?
DON'T MAKE IT AGAIN.

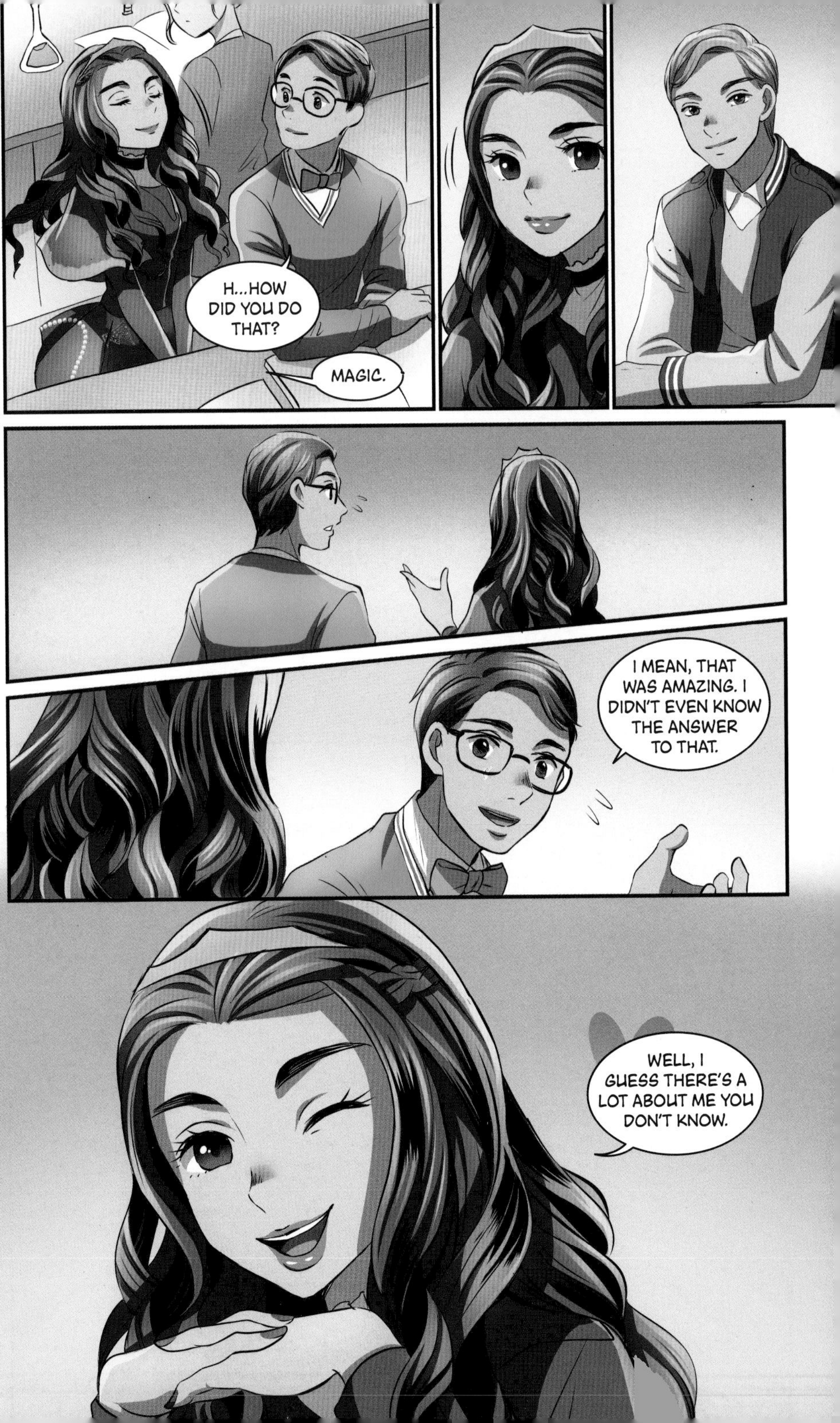
H...HOW DID YOU DO THAT?
MAGIC.
I MEAN, THAT WAS AMAZING. I DIDN'T EVEN KNOW THE ANSWER TO THAT.
WELL, I GUESS THERE'S A LOT ABOUT ME YOU DON'T KNOW.

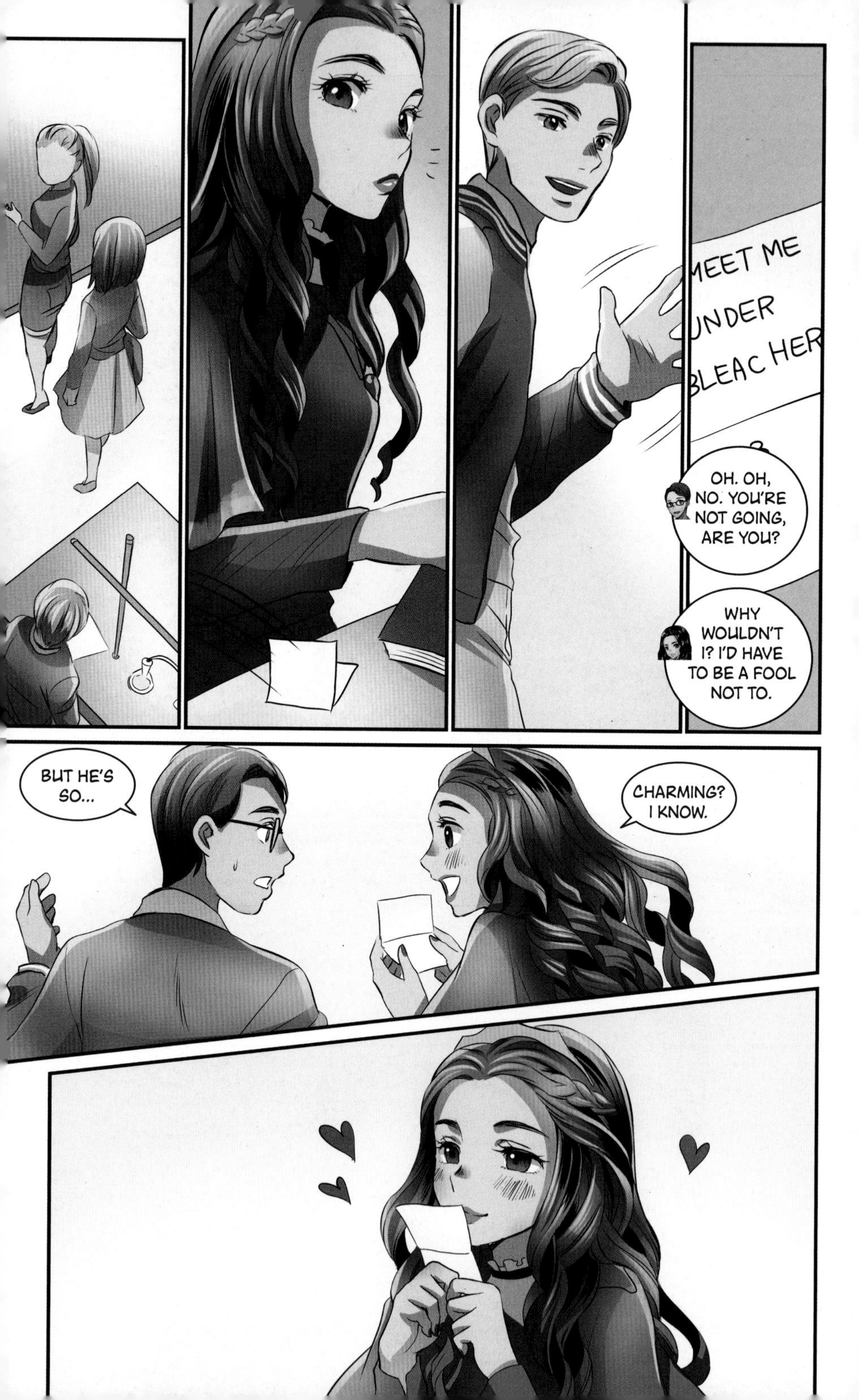
MEET ME
UNDER
BLEACHER
OH. OH, NO. YOU'RE NOT GOING, ARE YOU?
WHY WOULDN'T I? I'D HAVE TO BE A FOOL NOT TO.
BUT HE'S SO...
CHARMING? I KNOW.

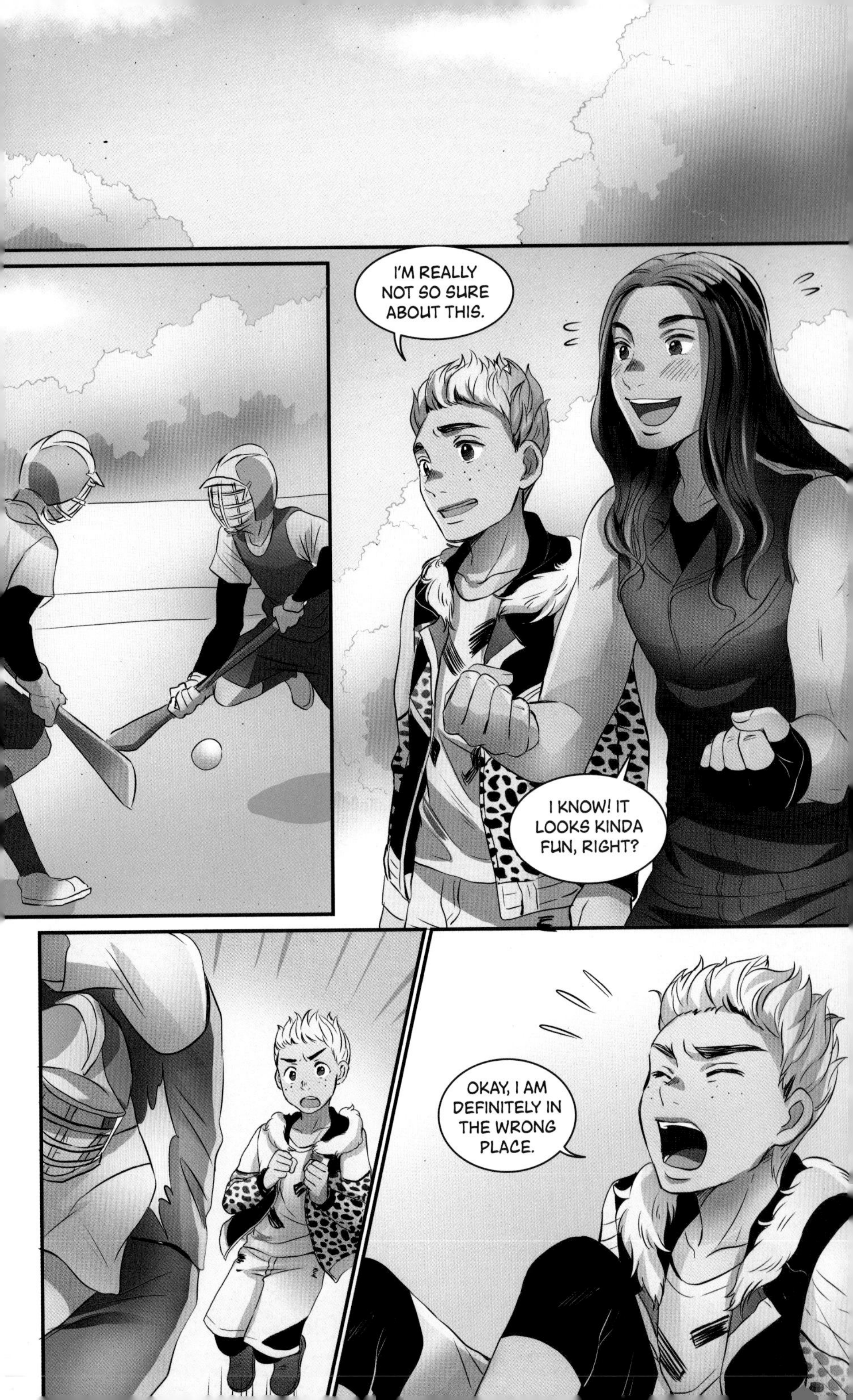
I'M REALLY NOT SO SURE ABOUT THIS.
I KNOW! IT LOOKS KINDA FUN, RIGHT?
OKAY, I AM DEFINITELY IN THE WRONG PLACE.

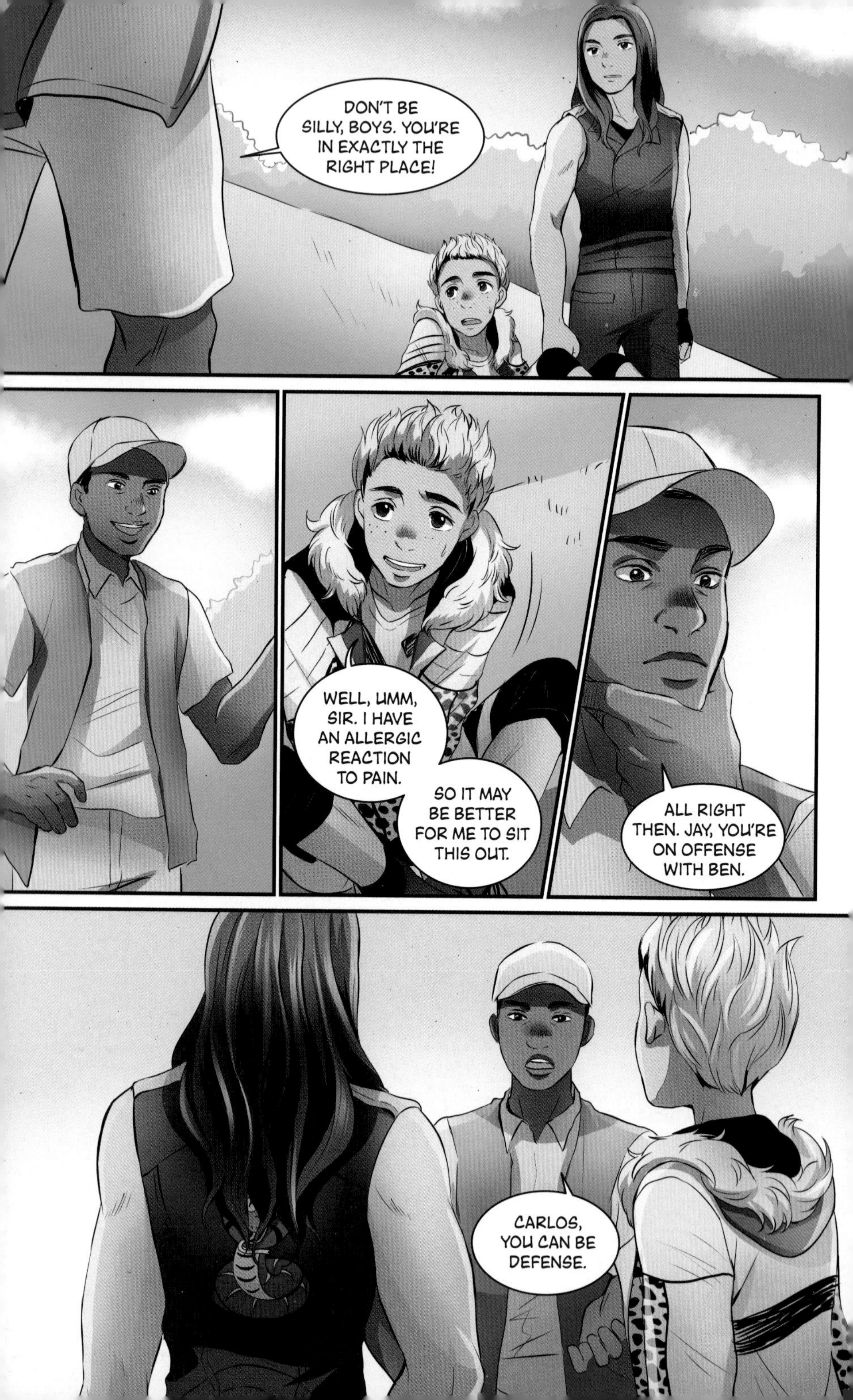
DON'T BE SILLY, BOYS. YOU'RE IN EXACTLY THE RIGHT PLACE!
WELL, UMM, SIR. I HAVE AN ALLERGIC REACTION TO PAIN.
SO IT MAY BE BETTER FOR ME TO SIT THIS OUT.
ALL RIGHT THEN. JAY, YOU'RE ON OFFENSE WITH BEN.
CARLOS, YOU CAN BE DEFENSE.

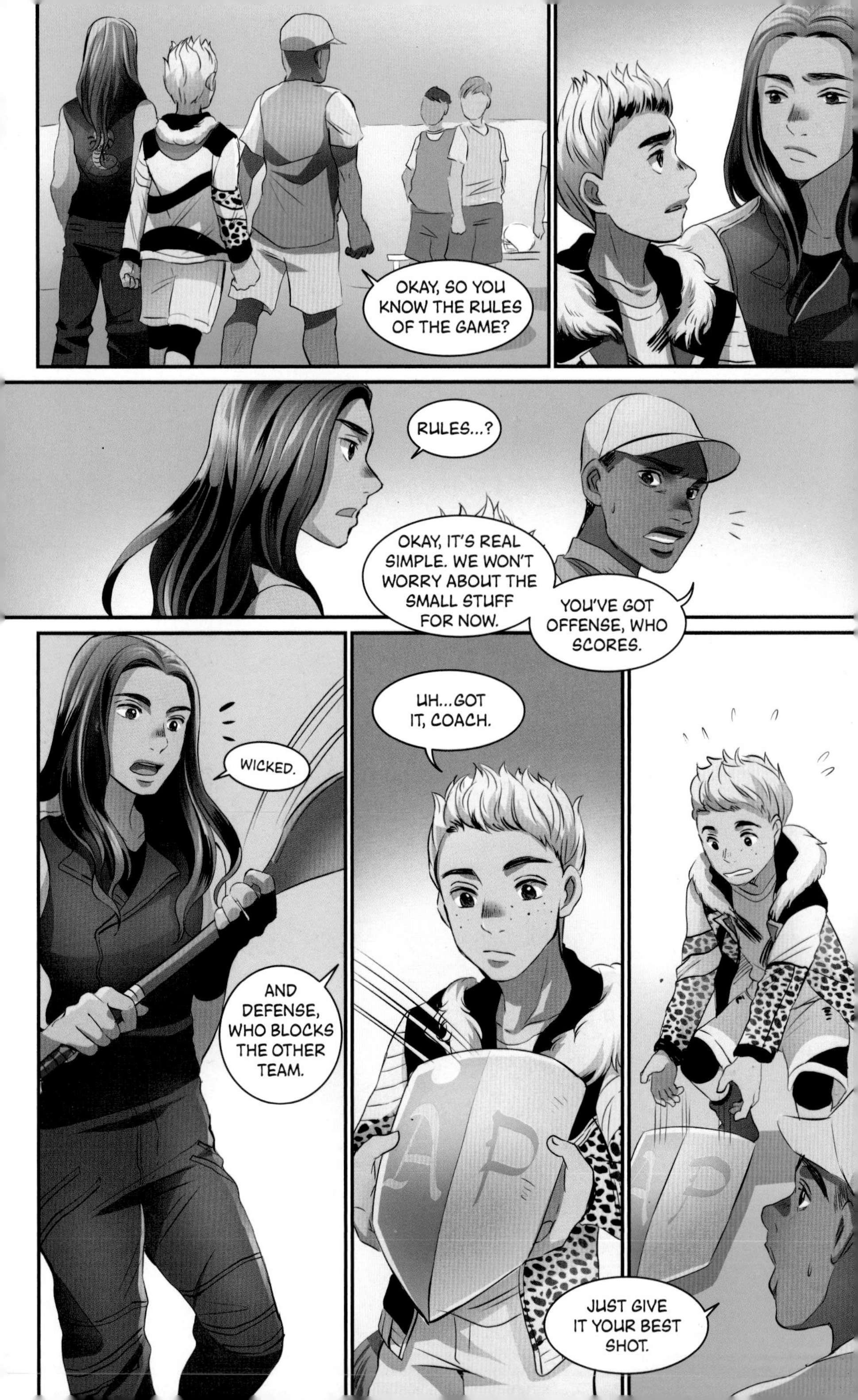
OKAY, SO YOU KNOW THE RULES OF THE GAME?
RULES...?
OKAY, IT'S REAL SIMPLE. WE WON'T WORRY ABOUT THE SMALL STUFF FOR NOW.
YOU'VE GOT OFFENSE, WHO SCORES.
WICKED.
AND DEFENSE, WHO BLOCKS THE OTHER TEAM.
UH...GOT IT, COACH.
JUST GIVE IT YOUR BEST SHOT.

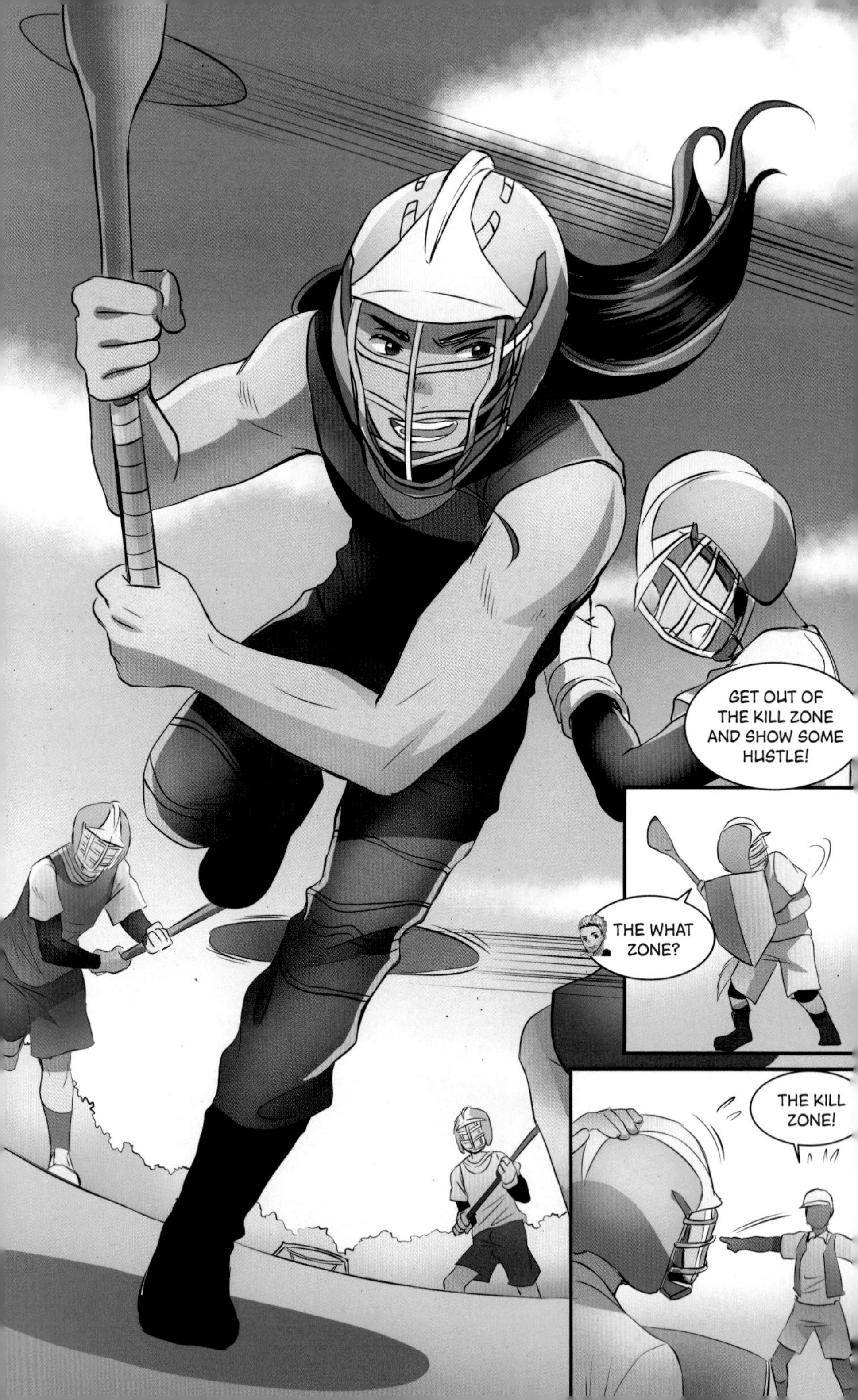
GET OUT OF THE KILL ZONE AND SHOW SOME HUSTLE!
THE WHAT ZONE?
THE KILL ZONE!

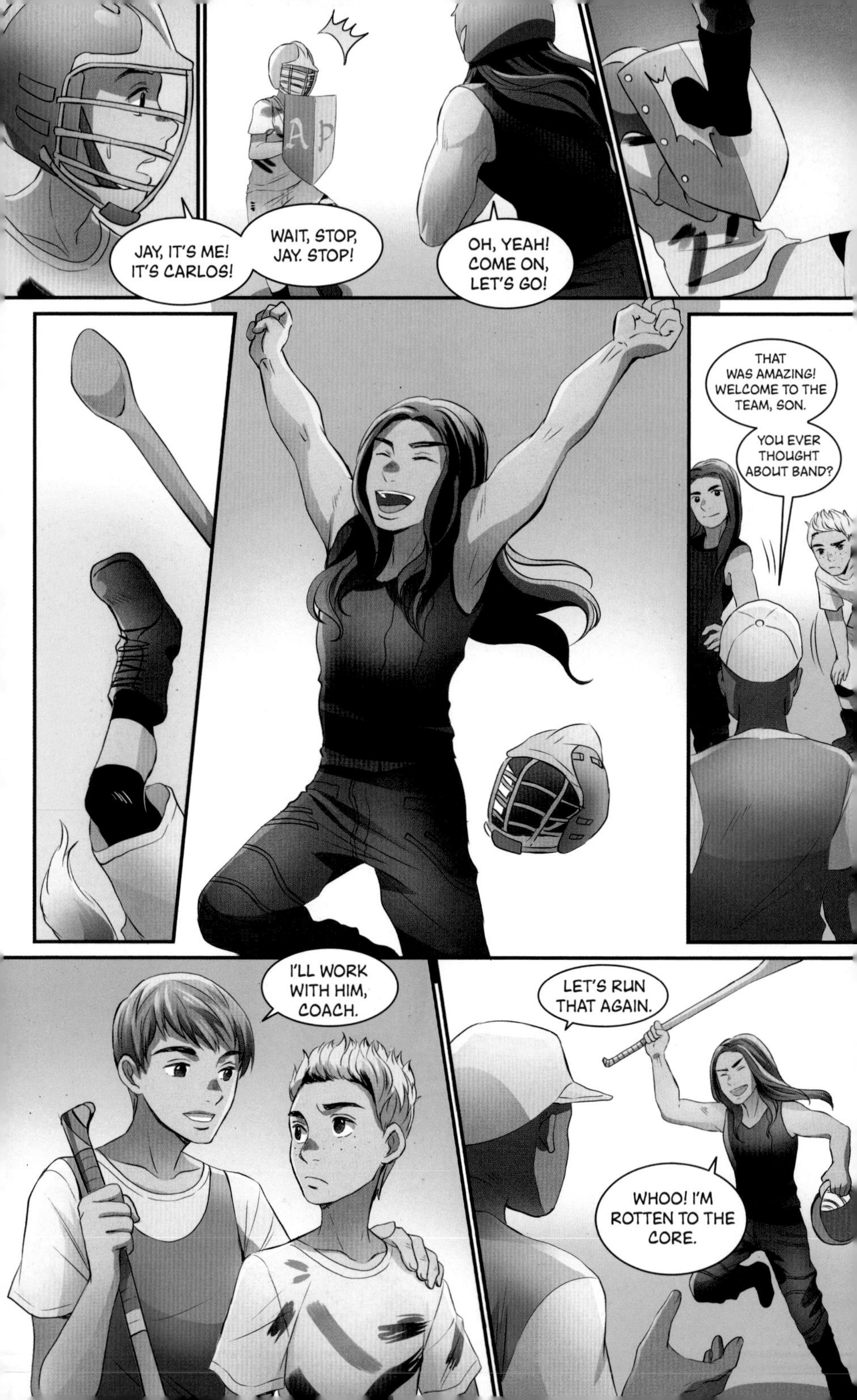
JAY, IT'S ME! IT'S CARLOS!
WAIT, STOP, JAY. STOP!
OH, YEAH! COME ON, LET'S GO!
THAT WAS AMAZING! WELCOME TO THE TEAM, SON.
YOU EVER THOUGHT ABOUT BAND?
I'LL WORK WITH HIM, COACH.
LET'S RUN THAT AGAIN.
WHOO! I'M ROTTEN TO THE CORE.

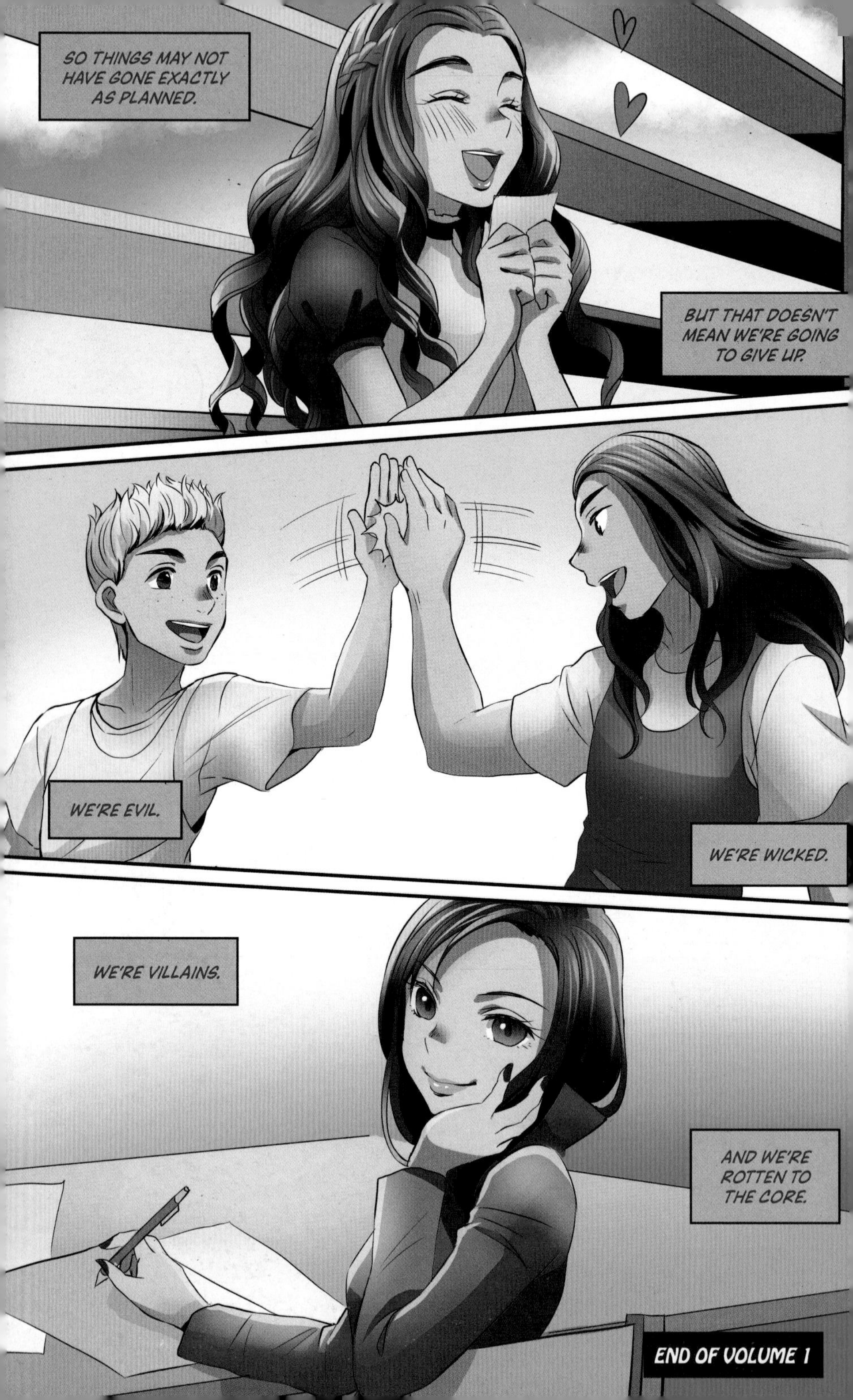
SO THINGS MAY NOT HAVE GONE EXACTLY AS PLANNED.
BUT THAT DOESN'T MEAN WE'RE GOING TO GIVE UP.
WE'RE EVIL.
WE'RE WICKED.
WE'RE VILLAINS.
AND WE'RE ROTTEN TO THE CORE.
END OF VOLUME 1